JIMMY THE FREAK

Charles Colyott & Mark Steensland

BLOODSHOT BOOKS

READ UNTIL YOU BLEED!

ALSO BY CHARLES COLYOTT

Black - Canto I of The Nephilim Codex
Unknown Pleasures

The Randall Lee Mysteries
Changes
Pressure Point
Jianghu
Eating Bitter

ALSO BY MARK STEENSLAND

The Special (with James Newman)
In the Scrape (with James Newman)
Behind the Bookcase
Autumn Prose, Winter Verse

I

There's something almost magical about it, Mike thinks, watching the fat flakes of snow appear from a sky black as the void. It's really starting to come down. The snow swirls in thick spiraling currents, an unsullied virginal white until they hit the cone of sodium vapor streetlight where the flakes become molten sparks. And there, standing in the brilliant cone of light, is Jimmy, his massive head thrown back, his mouth open.

He's grinning.

And the thing about Jimmy is ... well, seeing him standing out in the parking lot would be enough to scare the shit out of almost anybody. Mike wasn't exactly a shrimp, himself, but he looked like a dwarf next to Jimmy, who was not only taller but a good 70 pounds or so heavier. Jimmy was built like one of those masked killers in the movies, the guys who always seemed to wait for a chick to take her top off before whacking her with a hatchet or something. What ruined the psycho image, what absolutely destroyed the whole serial killer vibe, was Jimmy's face. It was a bit like seeing a five-year old's grin plastered on a 30-something-year-old's face.

Mike stood at the window and watched the kid (and he couldn't help that was how he thought of Jimmy, even though they were close in age). He was catching snowflakes on his tongue, grinning all the while. For a second, Mike thought maybe he'd been grinning, too, but then the magic was gone. No real reason, either. One minute the world had been a warm, fair place and now it wasn't. Never had been, really.

The phone was ringing. It was louder than any phone had a right to be, especially in this thin-walled shithole. And when the phone finally stops ringing, it's like the rest of the world rushes in--the roar of traffic on the freeway, the infomercial on the TV, the constant mosquito buzzing whine of the neon sign outside.

The colors flash in gaudy red and blue. It's supposed to read Sandman Motel and Always a Vacancy! but with about half the letters burned out, the only thing the sign was really good for was instigating a migraine, as it was now.

Squeezing his eyes closed, Mike rubs at his temples hoping to ease the thing before it really gets a foothold.

Instead there's a pounding on his door to match the one in his head.

Through the peephole he sees her, all sagging flesh and varicose veins crammed into some kind of floral print sack, hair rolled in pink curlers. It is the same shade of pink as that sugar-free sweetener, the shit that supposedly gives rats cancer.

He draws back from the peephole and silently mouths a curse.

"I know you're in there. I seen your car. And this ain't walkin' weather. You best be paid in full by tomorrow or I'm callin' the cops."

She pounded on the door one last time before the cold drove her back to the office. Mike pulled back the thin maroon curtain and watched the old woman hobble along with the aid of a quad cane which sported split tennis balls on each of its spider-like feet.

With a sigh and a full bladder, he turned from the window and went to take a leak. After flushing the toilet and washing his hands, he caught sight of a teddy bear in the bathtub. One of its eyes was gone and a tuft of cotton poked from the hole.

Mike swore to himself again and grabbed his coat.

After checking the window again to make sure the manager was for sure back in her office, Mike crept out of his room and did his best to stick to the shadows as he moved across the lot toward the hulking form crouched on the wet ground.

The kid had stopped catching snowflakes. Now he was scraping his hands on the pavement, trying to get enough snow together to make something resembling a snowman. What he managed was a small mound of sooty slush with twigs poking out at odd angles.

"Jimmy, don't lick your lip, man. C'mon. What did I tell you about that?"

Jimmy looked at Mike, his tongue still tracing his moist upper lip.

"You said don't. I remembered."

"Yeah, but you're still doing it."

"Sorry, Mike."

And he was. His eyes were downcast as he drew his sleeve across his face, wiping his mouth and nose in one massive swipe.

"C'mon, man. We gotta get you inside. You're freezing your ass off, aren't you?"

Jimmy grinned again and bobbled his head senselessly in a motion that was neither yes or no.

"I'm buildin' a snowman, Mike! You wanna help me build a snowman?"

Mike scowled and shook his head.

Jimmy's grin faded. "You always shake your head, Mike."

"Maybe tomorrow, all right?"

"Really?"

"Sure."

"Promise?"

"Yeah. Maybe. I dunno. C'mon. It's fuckin' freezing out here. You gonna tell me you aren't cold? Look at you."

He offers Jimmy his hand, to help him up, but the gesture is mostly politeness. Jimmy's hand closes around Mike's, engulfing it. The massive hand is ice cold, perfectly smooth, with surprisingly soft skin, and although Mike is fairly certain Jimmy could smash his hand with minimal effort, he doesn't. The kid barely squeezes at all, in fact, instead only using the grip as leverage to get his feet underneath him.

Nobody would call him graceful, but as Jimmy rose to his full height, Mike was grateful that at least the kid knew his own strength.

Once they were inside, Mike took Jimmy to the bathroom, turned on the hot water, and tried to rub some life into his frozen hands. At first, Jimmy tried to pull away. It had to hurt, Mike thought. Finally, though, Jimmy stopped fighting and let his hands remain under the steaming faucet.

"Too hot?"

Bobble.

"Feeling any better?"

Bobble.

"Y'know, you're lucky. What if you got frostbite, hunh? What then?"

"What's frostbite, Mike?"

"It's where your shit gets all froze up, man. Then a doctor cuts off your fingers. You want that?"

He bobbled his head again, but his wide, fearful eyes told Mike more than the incoherent movement.

"Damn right, you don't. So don't do it anymore. You want to play outside, you gotta wear your coat and you gotta wear your gloves. Right?"

"Okay."

The kid's nose is still bright red and runny. Mike sees the tip of Jimmy's tongue emerging from the corner of his mouth.

"Aw, c'mon! Don't lick your lip. You'll get all chapped again. Plus, you got snotnose. You don't want to lick up a bunch of snot, do you?"

As Jimmy's head bobbles again, Mike grabs a towel from the rack and dries Jimmy's hands. The he flips it over and wipes Jimmy's nose.

"Why don't you go grab your coat."

"Are we gonna build the snowman now?"

"Nah, you're still half frozen."

"Pizza?"

"No. Money."

"Then pizza?"

"You, always with the pizza. Just get your jacket."

Mike grabs his keys from the nightstand and shrugs into his jacket as Jimmy walks past him, carelessly flinging the door open. In an instant, Mike is there, wincing as he shoulders the door closed. He raises a finger to his lips.

"You gotta let me check first. Then we're gonna go quick and quiet as we can, sticking to the shadows, all right? We're going past the car, to the street. And no fuckin' around. Got it?"

"Are we playing spies again, Mike?"

"Sure, sure. There's a ... a sentry. Out by the corner. And if she sees us, Jimmy, it's gonna be a bad night."

Jimmy nods seriously and crouches. In a crouch, he's roughly the same height as Mike.

Opening the door a bare few inches, Mike scans the lot. He can see the blue flicker of a television through the office window and says a silent prayer that it's enough.

"Ready?" He says.

Jimmy nods again, muscles coiling like springs.

"Go!" He says, opening the door. Jimmy runs along the shadows of the motel for as long as he can before executing a clumsy and completely unnecessary roll on his way past the car. Mike swears under his breath and follows. Without the roll.

Once they've crossed the street and are safely away from the manager's view, Mike lights a cigarette and, from the corner of his mouth, says, "That was real good, Jimmy."

"Hey, Mike?"

"Yeah?"

"Where we goin'?"

Mike exhales a lungful of smoke. "To get some money, remember?"

"Oh. Yeah. And pizza, right?"

"We'll see."

In spite of the few blocks to the convenience store, Mike finds himself shivering deeply. The night air is that particular breed of damp cold that seeps directly into the bones, the sort his grandfather used to feel coming from a mile away in his rheumatic joints.

He looked over to see how the kid was doing.

Jimmy was busy trying to make smoke rings with the steam of his breath, with varying degrees of success.

"Look, Mike!"

"Yeah, I'm lookin,' Jimmy. That's real good. You see the store?"

"Sure."

"That's where we're going. Now I need you to pay attention."

"How'm I supposed to pay attention if we don't have any money?"

Mike stops, turning to stare at Jimmy.

Jimmy's face is a mask of concern except for one corner of his already chapping mouth, which twitched wildly before breaking into a grin.

A joke. The kid told a joke.

"I heard that one on the TV. Pretty funny, huh?"

Mike allows himself a tired smile and says, "Yeah, bud. That's a good one. Real funny. You ready?"

"Born ready. Just like you."

"Remember: hundred bucks or less. Otherwise we can't collect."

Jimmy nods with what Mike could swear was annoyance playing across his features.

"I know, I know."

Mike pulls the convenience store door open. The warm air, thick with an olfactory cocktail of coffee, nearly petrified hot dogs, and industrial cleaning fluids, caressed his face, beginning the process of thawing it. He stepped inside, making room for Jimmy. As they stomped the slushy snow from their shoes, Mike saw the two clerks staring at them so he returned the favor. Hard.

The clerks were a couple of dopey college kids, most likely, and that was good, but Mike saw an older guy in the back, counting a register drawer.

Mike caught up to Jimmy, who was already in the candy aisle, and elbowed him gently in the side. Jimmy looked over blankly, his eyes scanning the counter.

"We got a supervisor in the back, too."

Jimmy smiled. "I know."

Of course he did.

Jimmy holds up two packages. One is chocolate-covered peanut clusters; the other, neon-colored gummy worms. He smiles hopefully.

Mike raises a single finger and says, "One. You can have one. But you have to pick."

"But they're different, Mike. And they're both good, only in different ways."

"One."

The big man's smile fades and he stares at the packages in his hands.

Mike leaves him to his deliberations and approaches the translucent case on the counter, idly leaning forward to study the colorful rolls of scratch-off tickets inside. Jimmy joins him a moment later, and the nearly constant bobbling motion of his head ceases. He raises one thick finger slowly.

"Can I help you?" One of the clerks, an acne-plagued redhead said. His name tag read Greg.

Mike straightens, turns, and says, "Hey, you guys got any cream soda?"

From the corner of his eye, he sees the other clerk, a tall black kid named Ronnie, checking them out. He's frowning a little, and Mike knows that look. He knows something isn't on the up-and-up, but he doesn't know what. It could be enough to cause problems, though, and they didn't need another problem right now.

"In the back with the rest of the drinks," the suspicious clerk, Ronnie, says.

Mike offers an embarrassed smile. "Yeah? Y'know, it's not always so easy to find these days. I guess everybody buys those energy drinks."

The clerk stared at him.

"I really hate to bother you," Mike said, "but I left my glasses at home. Do you think you could show me where they are? I can't see a foot in front of my face without my glasses."

Ronnie stares at him for a second and lets out a long, slow breath. Then he steps out from behind the counter and leads Mike back to the cooler.

He waves a disinterested hand at one of the cooler doors and says, "There you go. Third shelf," before turning to head back to his post.

Mike sees Jimmy standing near the counter, his body perfectly still. He cannot see Jimmy's face, but he knows what Greg is seeing.

"Hey ... Hey! Are you okay, man?"

"You got any two-liters of the stuff?" Mike said, distracting the clerk again. "What?"

"Any two-liters? Cream soda?" He says again.

The clerk walks behind Mike and grabs one from the display on the floor. "Here. What's going on with your friend?"

Mike looks around the clerk with concern. Then he flashes an awkward and apologetic smile. "Oh ... it's called a petit mal seizure. He gets them sometimes. Part of his ... condition. His mom dropped him when he was a baby."

Pushing carefully past the clerk, Mike makes his way to Jimmy just as the kid takes a long, shuddering breath and seems to return to his body.

"You got it?" he asks, and the kid nods.

Mike flashes the same apologetic smile to Greg, and hands him the two-liter bottle of cream soda.

"Lucky 21," Jimmy says, beside him. "Lucky 21."

Still smiling at the clerk, Mike says, "I guess we'll take a scratcher, too. The, uh, Lucky 21."

The clerk reaches into the case, tears the ticket from the roll, and slides it across the counter to Mike as Greg adds it to their total.

"$2.89," Greg says.

Mike fishes three crumpled bills from his pocket and tosses them on the counter. The clerk takes each and smoothes it flat before slipping them into the register drawer with a vague look of disdain. He slides Mike's change--a dime and a penny--to him.

Using the penny, Mike scratches off the ticket and chuckles. "Hey! Will you look at that? A hundred bucks!"

"No kidding?" Ronnie asks. Now both clerks are staring at them with renewed interest. Mike smiles, though he feels sweat pooling on the back of his neck and along his ribs.

Ronnie studies the ticket for a minute, then looks up. "You weren't kidding." Turning, he says, "Hey, Chuck?"

From the back office, a voice says, "Yeah?"

Ronnie goes to the office, still holding their lottery ticket. Mike watches him and takes a long breath.

"Why did he do that?" Jimmy whispers beside him.

"What?"

"Why did he do that?"

"Why did who do what?"

"Him! Him! Why would he take money from the register? Supposed to put it in, but he took it out. $20. He took $20."

"No he didn't. He gave me my change, that's all."

"Not him," Jimmy says. Turning, he points at the other clerk, Greg. "Him."

"What?" Greg asks, a note of defensive anger in the question.

"Nothing," Mike said, quickly.

But Jimmy was putting his finger in the clerk's face, leaning over the counter with a steely j'accuse look that would've been comical in another circumstance, one that wouldn't get them busted.

"You took $20," the big man hissed.

Mike tried to get between Jimmy and the counter but only succeeded in placing himself in the kid's field of vision, which might have been enough.

"No, Jimmy, he didn't. He didn't even handle the change. The other guy did."

At that moment, Ronnie returned with their prize money, a crisp new one-hundred-dollar bill. Mike snatched it from his hand and scooped up the cream soda.

"You want a bag?" the clerk asked.

"Nah, we're good. I gotta get the big guy home. He's overdue for his meds."

He grabbed Jimmy by the coat and ushered him to the street.

Once they were clear of the windows, Mike picked up the pace, half-dragging Jimmy.

"Did we do good?" Jimmy said.

"Yeah, kid. Real good." He looked over his shoulder, saw the convenience store's door swing open and the defensive clerk stepping out, looking directly at them. Under his breath, Mike swore.

"Then why are you swearing?"

"You shouldn't have read that guy."

"Couldn't help it. He cut in on me. You know what happens when people cut in on me."

"All right, all right. We just need to get moving is all."

Looking back toward the mini-mart, he felt a rush of relief because the clerk was no longer there.

He didn't see that the man had moved into the shadows and was following them.

2

Bony old hands counted the change onto the yellowed guest register. Mike glanced at the hotel manager's face, contorted into what was probably supposed to be a kindly grin. He thought she looked like the Crypt Keeper from that old TV show.

"...and 18 makes 100. Thank you, Mr. Smith."

"Thank you, ma'am," he said, pocketing his change. "And, uh, sorry for the trouble."

"No trouble now," she said, face stretching tighter, showing off teeth the color of water damage.

After they left the office, Jimmy said, "She don't like me."

"Who, the manager?"

Jimmy nodded.

"Why do you say that?"

Jimmy looked at his battered shoes.

Mike fished the room key from his pocket and slid it into the lock on their door.

"You weren't reading her, were you?"

"Sorry, Mike."

Sudden anger filled him then, and he grabbed Jimmy by the sleeve of his coat and shoved him through the open door. He followed the now cowering giant and slammed the door shut.

"Do you want to die? Is that it?"

"No!" Jimmy said, trying to back away, but Mike was faster. He backed Jimmy into the wall and shoved his index finger into his ear. When he drew the finger out, it glistened red.

"Look. Look."

Jimmy stared at the bloody finger and his breath hitched pathetically.

"You're doing too much. You know what happens. You gotta give it a rest, all right?"

Jimmy nodded.

With an exasperated sigh, Mike flipped on the TV and gestured to a spot at the end of the bed for Jimmy to sit. An old Popeye cartoon is on a staticky public access station, and that's good enough for Jimmy. It's like nothing happened at all.

Mike sat down at the small table in the corner of the room and counted out their money. They didn't have much, not enough to last the week. And what was he supposed to do, get a job? Who would watch the kid? He rubbed his tired eyes and let out a long breath.

Jimmy would have to do it again.

And he would. Happily.

He wouldn't remember his old buddy Mike screaming in his face, telling him he was going to die if he kept it up. He wouldn't remember the bloody finger, he never did.

"We get pizza now?" Jimmy said. Mike turned to look at him, at his big, goofy grin and the often-disconcerting way his head bobbled as if on a loose spring. He forced himself to smile back.

"We got the cream soda, right? And like you always say, cream soda and pizza go together like Mike and Jimmy, right?"

"That's right, pal," Mike said, swallowing the lump in his throat. He had to remind himself that this money was Jimmy's, really. If the kid wanted pizza then by God he was getting pizza.

Jimmy was grinning like a lunatic and bouncing on the bed as Mike called the first delivery place he could find in the yellow pages.

"Yeah, we're gonna need this delivered--Jimmy! Knock it off, bud, you're gonna break the bed. I--What? ... Wait, what? No, but your ad says you deliver."

Looking at Jimmy, practically frozen in mid-jump, face fallen, Mike felt an odd mixture of emotions. There was something undeniably comical about the kid's expression, but something so terrible there, as well. Jimmy looked pained.

"Look, pal, nobody else delivers out this way. I'll make it worth your while."

Jimmy pathetically mouthed the word pizza with exaggeration: "PEEEEEEZZZZZZAAAAAAHHHHH."

Mike sighed and, to the clerk on the phone, said, "Yeah, all right. I'll pick it up."

Jimmy thrust his fists into the air, an emphatic V for Victory, and began jumping on the bed again with renewed enthusiasm.

Seeing Jimmy's face, Mike broke out in a matching grin.

3

Greg stood outside the auto shop. The exterior lights were off, and the dim glow seeping from beneath the door wasn't enough to show him the burly dude who was blocking his way. All he knew was: it wasn't Tony. Tony wouldn't have been such a dick.

"Look, man, I'm freezing my ass off. Let me in. I need to see him right the fuck now."

"He's busy."

Greg sighed, expelling a thick cloud. "Why don't you go ask him if he still wants the money Greg owes him."

The big man seemed to consider it for a long moment before saying, "Hold on."

Left to himself, Greg blew into his hands and used the minimal warmth to thaw his bare arms. Like an idiot, he'd left his jacket back at the Quickstop.

The door opened again and the burly dude (whose name, according to a patch on his overalls, was Pat) waved him inside.

4

"**I** got it, Mike. Really."

Mike zipped his jacket and said, "Then tell it back to me."

Jimmy looked at the ceiling and his mouth went momentarily slack.

"Stay in the room."

"Right."

"Don't go outside."

"Right."

"No more snowmen."

"That's right, Jimmy."

"Not tonight, but tomorrow maybe."

"Right. What else?"

"No answering the door."

"Right."

"But what if it's the pizza guy? What if he changed his mind?"

Mike stared at him. "Is that a joke? You joking again, Jimmy?"

Jimmy smiled and nodded.

"That's a good one. But do you want this pizza or not?"

Jimmy stood and grabbed Mike's shoulders. With perhaps one percent of his strength, he shook Mike like a rag doll. "YESSS. WHAT ARE YOU EVEN WAITING FOR? GO GET IT."

18   JIMMY THE FREAK

He tried to hide his grin, but Mike had to admit that sometimes hanging with the kid was all right. He turned to remind Jimmy of the rules but stopped himself. Jimmy knew. They'd been over it a hundred times by now. Instead, he flashed the kid a grin and a salute and made sure the door was locked on his way out.

5

Fluorescent shop lights illuminated a brilliant rectangle in the middle of the garage. Outside the glare lay only blackness. Greg thought he could see more guards standing around, but he couldn't tell how many. Beneath the lamps, seated around an old card table covered with black marker graffiti, were a group of men playing poker. The one who looked at him first--the man he'd come looking for, in fact—was the sort of guy whose photo showed up next to the entry for "Trouble" in the dictionary.

Sam Kochanak wasn't abnormally tall, or sculpted from slabs of muscle, but he may as well have been. With his gleaming bald pate, carefully groomed goatee, and the intense black and grey tattoo that took up most of his neck, the man looked a bit like Anton LaVey after a stint of hard time in Rikers.

As Greg told Kochanak what he'd seen in the Quickstop, Sam lit a cigarette. His eyes didn't leave Greg's the entire time, turning the clerk's guts sour.

"Are you fucking shitting me?"

Greg swallowed hard and said, "You think I'd come and interrupt your game for nothing?"

"For your sake I hope not."

"I'm not bullshittin' man."

Sam took a long drag from his cigarette and leaned back in his chair. "So you're saying what, exactly? This guy's got a psychic retard? That's what you're telling me?"

Greg had to admit that the whole thing sounded a little ridiculous when he put it that way, but he had to see this through, now. If Sam didn't buy the story, well, he didn't want to think about that.

"Look, all right? I got in around noon. I owed you fifty from the thing last week. I also wanted to try and pick up a sixer for tonight. So, first customer, he asks for a couple packs of Kools. I handed him the smokes, hit the no sale on the register, made like I was giving him his change, and I pocketed his twenty. This was noon, Sam. Nobody saw it, and I sure as shit didn't tell nobody. But this freak fuckin' knew. He looked right at me and he knew. I could see it, man. And then, as icing on the cake? He picked a winning scratch off."

"So fuckin' what? Half of those things pay out something, right?"

"No, not something. He picked one ticket. One ticket. And it won a hundred bucks."

Sam stared at him for a long moment, snakes of smoke writhing in the air between them. Then, stamping out his cigarette on the card table's already scarred surface, Sam stood.

"All right. Fuck it. Let's go."

6

Mike sat on the hard plastic bench and watched another customer stroll in and walk out with an order. After they left, Mike got up and approached the cashier.

"Listen, man: how much longer is this gonna be? I called my order in over 30 minutes ago."

The cashier did his best to appear sympathetic but it was obvious he was counting down to the end of his shift. "Just a couple minutes. Had to send a driver to the store for green peppers. We ran out."

"Then leave 'em off. I gotta get back. My kid brother's by himself." Mike had used the line before and it flowed smoothly from his lips. It even felt true. Hell, maybe it was.

"You sure?"

He nodded and checked his watch again.

15 minutes later, as he sat at the red light, waiting to pull into the hotel parking lot, the smell of pizza was driving him crazy. The snow had stalled out and the fat flakes fell now only in short bursts. He was watching them, waiting for the light to change, when he noticed the brake lights in the lot.

An SUV. Stopped in front of the hotel. Far end. Their end. Driver's side door hanging open.

"Dammit," Mike said. The road was clear, no traffic in sight, so he blew the red light, whipping the sedan into the lot and angling it behind the SUV.

In an instant, he's surveyed the scene. The door to their room is open. Outside, in front of the SUV stands the kid from the convenience store, the one Jimmy called a thief. Next to him is a rough looking bald dude with a neck full of ink. Then, in the open doorway, Jimmy, being roughly escorted outside.

As everyone turned to look at the new car that had boxed them in, Mike opened his car door and got out. As he strode toward the men, the bald dude with the neck ink took a step toward him. "Who the fuck do you think you--" he managed before Mike pulled the .25 Beretta from the shoulder holster under his jacket and put a bullet through the man's knee cap. The small pistol was fitted with a suppressor which brought the sound of the gunshot down to roughly the volume of a cap gun. The man's scream as he fell to the wet pavement was considerably louder.

The men holding Jimmy let go to reach for their own weapons. Mike shifted his weight, brought his arm around in one smooth movement and fired twice. The first shot hit one of the thugs high in the arm, actually spinning him on his heel. The second shot had been low, opening a ragged hole in the arch of the other thug's sneaker.

In his periphery, Mike detected movement. He turned, saw the clerk from the convenience store running, and calmly shot him in the ass. The kid face-planted into oily gray slush, both hands holding the wound in his butt cheek.

Mike scanned the area, moving to Jimmy's side as the group of would-be kidnappers writhed on the pavement.

"Any more of them, Jimmy?" Mike asked, helping him to his feet.

Jimmy shook his head, eyes filled with tears.

"Get our stuff together, okay? It's time for us to hit the road."

Jimmy sniffled, nodded, and hesitantly said, "Did you get the pizza?"

"Yes, I got the damned pizza. Now go!"

Jimmy looked past Mike to the rough-looking bald guy with the bullet in his knee. He pointed and said, "Mike? He has a lot of money and he is a very not-nice guy and if he's a very not-nice guy and got his money from doing bad things then it's okay for us to take, right? For our trouble, like you always say?"

Mike looked at the man on the ground and couldn't help a smile. "Why yes, Jimmy. I believe them's the rules."

While Jimmy collected their things, Mike walked to where the not-so-mean-looking-now dude was struggling to reach the .45 revolver that he'd fumbled as he fell. Mike stepped on the back of his hand and knelt down next to him.

"Who the fuck are you guys?" Sam said, craning his neck to look at Mike.

Mike pressed the still hot tip of the suppressor against the man's cheekbone and forced his face to the pavement.

"Good enough answer?"

Sam nodded feebly.

Mike reached into the man's pocket, ignoring the knife and pack of condoms to reach a fat roll of bills.

He heard Jimmy shuffling out of the room with their duffel bags on his shoulders. To him he said, "In the car. I'll be right there."

To the man on the ground, he said, "For your own good, I recommend forgetting the last few hours. Forget you ever saw us. Forget you ever saw him. That's not a threat. I'm a nice guy, believe it or not. But it ain't me you gotta worry about, understand?"

The guy on the ground nodded again, though of course he didn't understand. He just didn't want to suffer anymore. And that was something Mike knew too well.

He stood, kicked the man's .45 halfway across the parking lot, and backed away to the car. Once he was inside, he made sure Jimmy was buckled in correctly and then threw the car into reverse and slammed on the gas. He whipped the wheel and spun the car into the opposite direction before shifting into drive. As they peeled out, Jimmy looked inside the pizza box and said, "Hey! They forgot to put green on it!"

"They ran out of green," Mike said, checking the rear-view mirror. He could hear sirens in the distance. They needed to get themselves lost, fast.

"But I like green!"

"Next time, buddy, okay?"

Jimmy nodded and pulled a slice from the box, clearly disappointed.

Mike sighed and checked the mirrors again.

"You want a piece?"

"Maybe later, Jimmy."

"Aren't you hungry? I thought you were hungry."

"Not so much anymore, Jimmy."

Jimmy looked down at his slice and then back at Mike. "I'm sorry."

"What the hell are you sorry for?"

"Making you mad."

Mike glanced at the kid. He hadn't touched his pizza. After everything, now he wasn't going to eat?

"Jimmy, I'm not mad."

"Yes, you are."

"I'm not. Now eat before it gets cold."

"But you are. I can--" He stopped talking and took a bite. A massive, over-sized bite that encompassed half the slice. His cheeks ballooned outward and strings of cheese dangled from his pursed lips.

"You can what? What were you going to say, Jimmy?"

Mike wasn't a very Zen guy. He didn't give much thought to controlling his thoughts or emotions. When he'd seen the guys trying to grab Jimmy he hadn't felt much of anything. Annoyance, maybe. Resignation. Now he was struggling to control his temper. The anger was there, practically humming behind his eyes.

Jimmy looked away and struggled to swallow. "Nuffin'," he said quietly.

"Are you reading me?"

"No, Mike."

"Don't lie."

"Not lying." Jimmy sniffled.

"Yes, you are."

"Not," he said, almost petulantly.

Mike reached across and touched his index finger to the trickle of blood leaking from Jimmy's ear. He tried to show it to Jimmy, but the kid just looked away.

"How many times I tell you, Jimmy? What's Rule Number One? Hunh?"

"Not to read you," Jimmy muttered.

"Can't hear you."

"NOT TO READ YOU. Others okay, but only when you say. Not you, ever. On account of how your thoughts are yours and how, if you want me to know 'em you'll tell me so."

"That's right."

"Only you weren't telling me you were mad at me and anyway it's not fair because it wasn't my fault."

Mike sighed. Jimmy was drawing himself inward, like he was trying to disappear. The kid couldn't handle any kind of conflict, Mike knew, and it wasn't fair to do this to him, but it made him so damned angry. Mike could almost imagine the inside of his head the way he remembered his old apartment, from before. Neither place was in any kind of shape for visitors. He was afraid of what the kid would find if he went digging around, and he didn't like the fact that their arrangement was strictly an honor system kind of deal. If Jimmy wanted to take a stroll through his every memory, there wasn't shit Mike could do about it.

"Hey, Jimmy, I'm sorry, okay? You're right. It wasn't your fault."

Jimmy perked up a little, but his brow was still creased with worry.

"I did everything you said. I didn't open the door. They knocked, but I didn't open it and I didn't make a sound. They came in anyway and they found my hiding spot in the bathroom and I told them to leave me alone but they laughed at me and said no. And I yelled for you but you weren't there and so I was yelling for anybody to help but nobody did. But then finally you were there and you did." He extended his forefinger, making his hand into a make-believe gun and mimed firing. "BLAM BLAM BLAM BLAM! All fixed, just like before." He smiled at Mike and took a slice of pizza from the box. After taking an enormous bite, he said, "We need cream soda!"

"We got cream soda, remember?"

"I forgot it in the room."

Mike groaned.

"Anyway, it's okay because we forgot the candy corns and we have to have candy corns for dessert."

Shaking his head, Mike said, "We're gonna have to have a talk about nutrition one of these days, buddy."

7

Mike found a party-size bag of candy corn on a hook next to the other no-name-brand candy. All old-school stuff like wax bottles and candy buttons. The interior of the mini-mart was cold as fuck, and the store sound system was tuned to a station that apparently only played the kind of pop country bullshit that would've made Mike's grandpa spin in his grave.

Anxious to escape from this custom-designed personal hell, Mike looked everywhere for the cream soda, in vain.

The clerk, a bottle blonde chewing bubble gum and flipping through a fashion magazine, barely noticed his approach and made no attempt at customer service. "'scuse me," he said. "You guys got any cream soda?"

Without looking up, she said, "Cream soda? Never heard of it."

Mike stared at her. "Never heard of it?"

"Nope. What is it?"

"Eh. Y'know ... it's ... it's kinda like root beer."

"Nope."

"Is that nope you still don't know what I'm talking about or nope you don't have it?"

"Nah, I remember now, but if it's not back there, we don't got it." She looked at him for the first time, eyes framed with thick mascara. It was a child's makeup job, and Mike had to remind himself that she was, in essence, a child. She blew a small bubble and cracked it loudly.

He slapped the candy corn on the counter.

Once outside again, Mike felt a surge of panic when he didn't see Jimmy's silhouette in the car. He told himself that the kid had probably laid down, dozed off. Still, he quickened his step and felt the panic return after opening the door and finding the vehicle empty.

"Jimmy? Jimmy?!" he called. Mike scanned the streets, looking for any vehicles speeding from the scene, but there was nothing there. In the patchy, slushy snow, he saw one large, clear footprint and followed it like an arrow around the back of the building.

There, kneeling on the oily, wet pavement was Jimmy, scraping together the filthy slush into a loose pile.

Mike felt his body droop as the adrenaline flow abruptly shut off and his muscles relaxed. He took a few slow deep breaths to get himself under control before calmly saying, "C'mon, bud. I told you there's not enough snow for a snowman. You had me worried sneaking off, you know?"

Jimmy looked at Mike, his face blank, lined with shadow. He stood, slowly, and wiped hands on his jeans. "Sure," he said. "Tomorrow maybe. It's cold."

Mike nodded and offered what he hoped was a reassuring smile.

"Let's get you warmed up. We'll crank the heat and you can help me pick out our new hotel. How's that sound?"

Jimmy shrugged half-heartedly. "I'm tired, Mike."

"I know, buddy."

Mike let Jimmy doze while he drove. They'd have to ditch the car, of course, and he'd been listening to the police scanner app on his phone for over an hour, trying to track any potential problems.

He'd heard officers call in from the scene, minutes after they'd fled. From what had been broadcast over the scanner, it sounded like they were treating the incident as a robbery gone wrong. Good. Since one of the would-be kidnappers had tried to flee on foot, the genius investigating the scene put out an APB for suspects on foot. Mike was grateful for the slush. It didn't leave good, clear tire tracks. Still, he'd been careful. He'd driven two hours before stopping for Jimmy's beloved candy corn, and they went another 45 minutes before stopping for the night.

The strip was perfect. A long stretch of hotels, each a squat, bland fortress of mediocrity. Mike pulled into the parking lot of one of the hotels and parked behind the building where they wouldn't be visible from the road. After waking Jimmy, the two of them took their few belongings and walked almost a quarter of a mile down to one of the other hotels, the "Sunset Vista." Mike got their room, noticing how eerily similar this particular shithole was to the many other shitholes they'd stayed in. Different cheap wallpaper, different outdated carpet, same stale air, saturated with bargain cigarette stink.

By the time Mike got Jimmy settled, he fell into the room's lone queen-sized bed, pulled a rough starched sheet over himself, and blissfully ceased to be for a while.

8

Ash answered his phone before the second ring. "Yeah."

"Buffalo."

"You're sure?"

"Yep. Got into a gunfight with a batch of local low-renters."

Ash grinned. "Knowing our Mikey, I'm betting it wasn't much of a fight."

"Police report said he popped one of them in the ass as the chump tried to run."

Ash sat up, pushing aside the silk sheets with a laugh. "Sounds like our boy, all right. Tell me where to be."

He scribbled the address down on hotel stationery. He dressed in his finest suit, carefully adjusting his shoulder holster to make it lay flat, then placed the meticulously folded paper in his jacket pocket. Before leaving his suite, Ash glanced at his reflection in the mirror and smiled a wide, enthusiastic smile.

Today was going to be quite a day.

9

"Mike. Mike. Mike. Wake up, Mike. Mike. Miiiiiiiiiiiike."

Mike opened his eyes with a start, gasping. "Jesus H. Christ, Jimmy!"

"Mike, it's an emergency!"

"Jimmy, I just got to sleep, man. What's the emergen—Aw, for fuck's sake, Jimmy!"

The dark bullseye on the crotch of Jimmy's jeans ran all the way down one leg to his sock.

Jimmy blushed and said, "I'm real sorry, Mike. I had a dream I was peeing."

Mike sat up, rubbed his eyes, and said, "What do I always tell you, Jimmy?"

"'You pee in the dream, you pee for real.'"

"That's right. You gotta remember, and you gotta wake yourself up when that happens. BEFORE that happens, ideally."

Jimmy stared at him.

He sighed and said, "Okay, all right. It's over. Get undressed and I'll get you some clean clothes."

Jimmy started to go to their bags, but stopped abruptly. "Uh-oh," He said gravely.

Mike dropped his head into his hands and said, "Please tell me you're not shitting yourself now."

"Nooo. It's ... I was gonna tell you last night only you got so mad anyway and then later I forgot."

Realization dawned slowly in his sleep-deprived brain. Mike slumped. "Not again."

He got up, went to their duffel bags, and unzipped first one, then another. Inside, he pulls out a worn white towel. He turns and looks at a very sheepish Jimmy and pulls out another towel. And another.

"Dammit, Jimmy. You left everything?"

"Not the towels."

"The towels weren't fuckin' ours anyway. They don't belong to us. How many times have I told you this?"

The big man shuffled in place, clearly anxious, and his mouth moved soundlessly as he found the words. Finally, he simply said, "I was so scared, Mike." Then, as if on cue, he started to cry.

Mike took a deep breath. "C'mon, don't cry." Jimmy was working himself into a real fit. He'd seen it plenty of times before. "Stop it, Jimmy. Now."

Mike walked to the window, checked the parking lot and found it mostly empty.

"C'mon. We gotta go pick out some new clothes. Again."

Jimmy sniffled. "But I can't go out like this."

"Of course you can't. Get undressed."

10

The parking lot of the Wal-Mart was packed.

Of-fuckin'-course it is, Mike thought as he waited for a woman in a too-small tank top to drag her son out of their path. It seemed to take forever. As he pulled into the parking spot, Jimmy said, for approximately the four hundredth time, "Why can't I wait at the motel?"

"You know why," Mike said. Again.

"I forget."

"You can't stay because of what happened last night."

"You said you wasn't mad."

"I'm not, but I'm not letting it happen again. Now c'mon, let's get this over with."

"What about if I stay in the car?"

"No."

"Why not?"

Mike took a deep breath and let it out slowly. "Because if I pick out clothes for you, you're gonna complain about what I get."

"No I won't, Mike. I promise."

"'It's too scratchy, Mike!'"

Jimmy frowned and Mike knew that sometimes it took him a minute to access memories.

"That thing was SUPER scratchy, though, Mike."

"The point is, it's always something. Always. So you're gonna come with me, and you're gonna help. And then you can get dressed and we'll go on with the rest of our day. Okay?"

Jimmy frowned again, but nodded slowly.

They got out of the car, Mike in his slightly wrinkled and worn suit, Jimmy wearing nothing but Mike's overcoat, which fell to knee length on him. As a frigid breeze whipped through his bare legs, Jimmy groaned.

"But it's cold, Mike," he whined.

"You think I don't know that?"

Jimmy scowled at him. "Not as much as I know it."

"I guess you got that right," Mike said.

As they approached the entrance, the automatic doors slid open. Inside, an older guy welcomed them. He had too much pomade in his thinning hair, his greeter vest was gray around the edges, and his smile was far too enthusiastic smile. Once he got a look at Jimmy, knobby knees and all, the smile turned rancid on his face. Mike put his hand on the greeter's shopping cart and offered a smile of his own. The greeter stepped back from the cart, allowing Mike to take it. As he pushed the cart into the store, Jimmy followed, blissfully unaware of his appearance. Mike navigated his way to the men's department, occasionally reminding Jimmy that they weren't there to look at toys.

He checked sizes, then grabbed a pack of tee-shirts from the shelf. After clearing them with Jimmy, he tossed the shirts into their cart. He stepped away to grab some socks, and that was Jimmy's chance to look at the really cool hats across the aisle. Mike didn't notice. He was sorting through packs of socks. Glancing up, he saw a display of various underwear styles. Next to that was a clearance bin. Clearance was good. Any chance to stretch a buck meant using Jimmy less. "You want to try some boxers this time, Jimmy?"

He got no answer.

When he turned around, he saw that Jimmy had found some pants and was standing in front of a mirror, holding them against his waist to see how they looked. Problem was, the overcoat had come open. Without thinking about the consequences, Mike said, "Jimmy!"

Startled, Jimmy panicked, dropping the pants and spinning to face Mike. At the same time, with the sort of perfect synchronicity that God seems to find hilarious, a mother and her three young daughters turned the corner to come face-to-face with a very large, very naked man with a crazed look in his eyes. They all screamed. Of course they did.

II

"**A**ccidental indecent exposure?"

The store's security office was a small, squarish room with gray walls, a bulky old steel office desk decorated with ancient coffee rings, and a flickering fluorescent light that cast a dim yellow light on everything. It made the security officer look jaundiced. Or dead. Or both.

"Exactly. Like that Janet Jackson Superbowl thing. Remember that? They didn't put her in jail."

The security guard's dead face twisted into a sneer that was equal parts amusement and disgust. "Yeah, well, that's not Janet Jackson sitting out there."

Mike leaned forward, his fists on the steel desk. "No. He's a mentally handicapped individual who didn't understand what he was doing when he did it."

"Says you."

"You think he's, what, pretending? His mother dropped him on his fuckin' head in the bathtub when he was nine months old, okay? Look, man, I told you what happened. I told you why we were in here. And now I'm asking you to be a little decent. Please."

The security officer took a deep breath and leaned back in his chair, making it creak loudly. Mike watched him look out the office window at Jimmy, who tentatively raised a hand to wave.

The officer watched him for several long minutes. Mike resisted the urge to bite his nails.

"All right. I'm not unreasonable. You pay for the clothes, we'll let him use the office to get dressed, but I never want to have this conversation with you, or him, again. You understand?"

12

After Jimmy was dressed, Mike asked if they could exit through a back door. He was trying to leave the lightest trail possible and he didn't want to give anyone else a chance to remember them. Jimmy wasn't exactly inconspicuous, after all, even when he wasn't accidentally flashing people. Thankfully, the security officer complied. Mike promised he would never see them again as the door closed. Then he faced Jimmy and said, "This way."

Jimmy looked around, perplexed. "But isn't the motel that way?"

"We ain't going to the motel."

They were halfway across the parking lot, on the way to a brightly lit strip mall when Jimmy slowed down.

Mike kept walking, the neon glare of the store calling to him.

A car horn sounded loudly behind him, and he turned to see Jimmy standing in the middle of the road. He ran back to Jimmy, grabbed his arm and pulled him aside. He mouthed a sincere apology to the driver of the car that almost ran Jimmy down and received an equally sincere middle finger in return.

"What the hell are you doing?" Mike asked as the car sped past them.

Jimmy squinted hard and rubbed his eyes. "Reading the sign."

"The fuck's your problem. It says 'liquor store,' dummy."

The sudden hurt in Jimmy's wide eyes were a knife twisting in Mike's gut. "What did you say?"

"Shit, I'm sorry, pal. I didn't mean that."

"It's not a liquor store?"

"No," Mike said, even though he had the distinct impression that Jimmy was messing with him. "It's a liquor store."

"Then you're not going in there," Jimmy said, pulling his bottom lip over his top lip in an expression of smug superiority.

"I am. And you're coming with me."

"I don't like when you drink that stuff, and you said that you wasn't gonna. You said to remind you how you get."

"Look, Jimmy, I don't care how I get, all right? I'm not looking to get tanked, but it's been a shit couple of days, and I'd like to have a drink. A drink, okay?"

Jimmy pouted. "But I want pizza."

"Ugh, Jesus. I'm still picking the salami out of my teeth from the pizza we had last night."

Jimmy scowled. "Firstable, you shouldn't say 'Jesus' like that."

Mike blinked. He hadn't heard Jimmy use his version of "first of all" in a long time. The kid was pissed.

"And secondable, that one didn't have green on it. You said today we could have pizza with green on it."

"I said next time we had pizza it would have green on it."

Jimmy crossed his arms. "Last night you said tomorrow. And today is tomorrow."

"I said that about the snowman."

Jimmy brightened. "So we can build a snowman today?"

Mike felt the muscles between his shoulder blades knotting painfully. "Look. Let me get what I need in here and we can do whatever you want. Okay?"

Reluctantly, Jimmy nodded. Mike pulled open the door and ushered Jimmy inside.

13

Back at the motel, and with a half a paper cup of Jack Daniels sitting warmly in his gut, Mike made the call.

"Okay, I'm going to need you to repeat this back to me. I really need this pizza to be perfect tonight, cool? Okay, ready? I need pepperoni. Salami. Pineapple. Mushrooms. Olives. And green peppers. Lots of green peppers." Mike looked over at Jimmy. Jimmy smiled at him, giving his two thumbs up, and mouthed the word "PEEEEZZZZAAAAHHHHH."

After the pizza guy repeated the order and told them it would be delivered in 30 to 40 minutes, Mike said, "Perfect." He hung up the phone and reached for the fifth of Jack on the bedside table. He twisted the top off, filled the hotel's paper cup again, and drank the whole thing like a shot.

He didn't see Jimmy's smile fading.

14

The man called Ash pulled his black town car into the parking lot of the Sandman Motel. The drive to Buffalo had been pleasant enough, and he'd made excellent time. Along the way, the radio station had turned from smooth jazz to Christian contemporary to classical opera, and he let it be. He'd kept turning up the heat, though. The cold here was truly extraordinary.

As he got out of the car, the rapid change of temperature made his breath catch in his throat for a moment. He made his way to the manager's office. A sign on the door said they were "Closed Until Further Notice," but, seeing movement inside, Ash leaned closer to peer through the glass.

He knocked softly on the door.

The manager, an old woman with her hair in curlers and an ugly black eye, opened the door a crack. "Can't you read?"

Ash took a money clip from his pocket. "I'd like to rent a room that I do not intend to sleep in."

The old woman scowled and Ash noted fresh stitches in the woman's brow. They pulled taut as her papery skin flexed. "How's that?" She said.

Ash held up the money clip, fat with bills.

"I'd like to know about a pair of men who were here recently."

"Let me guess. You looking for the retard, too?"

Ash suppressed a wince and said, "That's right."

"You a cop or somethin'?"

Ash took out the money clip again and fanned several bills in his hand. "Shall we say I'm renting for two nights?"

The manager grabbed the money like a spider on a fly.

15

Mike tossed the pizza box onto the mustard yellow coverlet on the bed. "Yo, Jimmy? Pizza's here." Flipping open the lid, he said, "Come on, it's exactly how you like it. With red and yellow and fuckin' gray and black and green on it. Lots of green."

Mike looked around. It's not like the room is huge or anything, but until the pizza had come, he'd been preoccupied. Watchin' TV with his ole buddy Jack. Mike snorted a laugh.

Ole buddy Jack was the best.

Only now the kid was missing and that wasn't right. He was just fuckin' here, too.

Mike picked up the half-empty fifth of Jack and didn't waste time with the cup. He tipped the bottle and swallowed until the burn of the liquor made him take a breath.

He made his way to the bathroom and knocked on the door, but there was no answer.

"Jimmy? You in there? I know you gotta be in there."

The lock is cheap and shitty, one he could've popped with a screwdriver in two seconds. That didn't even matter, though, because the door was also cheap and shitty and the knob's bolt didn't line up with the strike plate, meaning the thing didn't latch at all. Mike shoved the door, admittedly a little harder than he meant to, and it flew open, startling the oversized manbaby who was huddled in the bathtub holding his Teddy bear in a death grip.

"Jimmy? What the hell, man? Didn't you hear me? I said your fuckin' pizza is here."

"I don't want it now," Jimmy said quietly.

"What?"

"I'll wait until later."

"No you will not. You rode my ass all damn day for this pizza, so you will come out here and eat it now."

Jimmy shook his head and squeezed his bear tighter.

"Now, Jimmy."

"Please, Mike. Leave me alone."

"Tell you what: I'm gonna think about all the things I'm going to do to you if you don't get your ass out of that tub and start eating this pizza. And then you can fuckin' read my mind. Because I'm sick of talking."

Mike turned away and sat heavily on the bed. Talking wasn't the only thing he was sick of. He was sick of taking care of the kid. Sick of the constant whining, the accidents, the routines that had to be followed to the letter. He's sick of shitty motel rooms that smelled like moth balls and stale jizz and mildew. Of cream soda and candy corn and fucking pizza. Of driving. Hiding.

Himself, too. He was sick of himself. Maybe that most of all. Weak, useless, and, deep down, mean.

"I don't see any cream soda or candy corns," Jimmy said from the doorway.

Mike looked at him in disbelief before shouting, "Because we don't have any, fucktard."

"I told you." Jimmy said.

"You told me what?"

"I don't like it when you drink that stuff."

"Yeah?"

Jimmy nodded and looked at his feet. "Yeah. This is what always happens."

"Oh, yeah? And what else happens?"

"Please, Mike. No. Don't."

In spite of Jimmy's pitiful tone--maybe because of it--Mike stood and started toward him, hands tightening into fists, but his feet were unexpectedly noodly, so he sat back down. "It's time we face facts, Jimbo. I gotta put you in a home somewhere. A place for people like you. Should have done that right from the start. I don't know what the fuck I'm doing."

Jimmy looked at him, his face concerned, but brighter. "Sure you do, Mike. You're keeping me safe. From Mister Bishop. Right?"

"For how much longer? He won't ever give up, Jimmy. He never gives up. Not when he really wants something."

"But you're better than him," Jimmy said hopefully.

Mike laughed bitterly. Jimmy started to laugh with him.

Mike slid the pizza box toward Jimmy and said, "Hurry up and eat. We're going out."

Jimmy smiled. "For cream soda and candy corns?"

"Not exactly."

16

Mike's sedan pulled into the gravel lot too cockeyed to fit any standard parking spot, even in a lot without painted lines. His right front wheel rode up on the yellow cement parking block, nearly tipping over the apex and rolling to the other side, which would've been a real bitch. Luckily, Mike reined it in, threw it in reverse, and let the wheel roll back to the earth with a hard thump.

Jimmy, clutching the dashboard with thick, sauce-stained fingers, stared wide-eyed at the women airbrushed onto the front of the building before them and said, "I don't wanna go in there."

"Why not?" Mike said, "Looks like a nice place to me."

He turned off the car and got out, somehow managing not to stumble on his way to the passenger side. As he opened the door, Jimmy repeated, "I don't wanna go in there, Mike."

Mike grabbed the kid by the tricep and used strategic pressure on the tendons to coax him from the car. "Yeah," he said, "well, too fuckin' bad."

The Velvet Kitten was covered--floor, walls, and ceiling--in red carpet that reminded Mike of cave mold. The music was painfully loud, especially for a Tuesday afternoon with less than a handful of patrons, and the bass rattled the fillings in his teeth. Black lights illuminated the stage, making the white bikini worn by the dancer glow an eerie blue as she twirled around a chrome pole. The place smelled like the cheap perfume worn by little girls playing dress up, all air freshener strawberry, vanilla, and rose. The stink of it hung in the air, waiting to cling to hair, clothes, the inside of the throat.

He made sure Jimmy was still behind him--the big goober looked like he didn't know left from right, though his eyes kept drifting to the blonde on the pole--and sidled up to the bar.

"What can I get you guys?" the waitress says with an impressive pillow of cleavage pushed up practically to her chin.

"Double whiskey for me, and for the kid--"

The waitress batted her eyelashes and waved a hand to the wall behind her like Vanna freakin' White showing off some valuable prizes. Mike saw what she was gesturing at and his heart sank.

"Sorry, sugar. We're totally virgin here. Even if we wasn't, though? Pretty sure I couldn't serve you anyway. You look like you've had plenty already."

Mike leaned on the bar, looked her square in the cleavage, and said, "If that's how you're gonna be, we'll have two cream sodas. But I expect cherries. And straws, dammit."

"Comin' right up."

Mike looked away from the waitress and back to Jimmy. He was smiling.

"They got cream soda?!"

"Yeah. Whoopdy-fuckin'-doo, eh?"

Mike scanned the room. Three stages, three dancers. A couple decent-looking cocktail waitresses.

Shit, he thought. Did you still call them cocktail waitresses when they didn't serve cocktails?

"All right, Copperfield. Which one of 'em thinks I'm cute. Somebody's gotta, right?"

"I don't know."

"So read 'em and see."

"You said not to."

"Yeah, but now I'm saying to."

"It's too noisy."

"That's bullshit and you know it."

Jimmy sighed and slumped on his stool. Closing his eyes, he immediately began to sweat. His eyelids fluttered, and a vein in his forehead throbbed.

"The dancing girls don't see you, they see shiny dollar signs." His hand rose, drawing the symbol in the air. Mike, though very drunk and annoyed, was often surprised by how simple and insightful the kid's gift could be. Even when the kid didn't know what he was looking at, his inner eye saw with 20/20 clarity.

Jimmy strained and cocked his head. "In the corner ... by the doors we came in. A waitress looked at you."

Mike frowned. "That's it?"

Jimmy shrugged and smiled a little. "She looked at you like I look at candy bars."

"Well, then. That might do. Oh, shit. Are we talkin' about the brunette?"

"Short, dark hair."

Mike was looking right at her as she took drink orders from a table of leering businessmen. She was petite. Athletic. Stacked.

"Yes! Good job, buddy. You got anything for me to work with?"

"Like what?"

"I dunno. Like last time. You remember that nice redhead in Boston? Gimme her favorite color. Or a favorite animal. Something. Whatever. Doesn't really matter."

Jimmy frowns, his brow furrowing. "Her name is Melinda."

"She's got a name tag, chief. I need something deeper."

"Deeper," Jimmy mumbles, and keeps reading.

The girl, Melinda, sauntered to the bar a few feet away from them. She glanced over as the bartender started to fill her order, and smiled, but there was nothing behind it. Mike smiled back and, under his breath, said, "Well?"

For anyone watching, the outcome of the ritual was never in doubt. The charming, well-dressed guy not only had money, he was also apparently taking his mentally challenged little brother out to a place where pretty ladies wouldn't laugh or sneer at him (not for a small fee, anyway).

It was clear the cute waitress thought the whole scheme was sweet. And she did indeed arrange for some of the girls to join the big fella at their table.

He was awful shy at first, but when one dancer (an Amazon named Cherry) showed off a small tattoo of a Pokémon on her hip, the two spent much of the rest of the night talking about their favorite episodes of the cartoon. On her break, the waitress joined them, and it was clear the well-dressed guy was buying her drinks.

By closing time, no one was surprised to see the cute waitress leaving with the well-dressed man, though a few were shocked to see Cherry kiss the big, goofy guy right on the lips.

None were so shocked as the big, goofy guy, though.

17

With dawn on the horizon and a hateful hangover looming, Mike struggled to fit the key into the keyhole as Melinda's mouth was all over him. Her hands were everywhere, and she was grinding against him in a way that made any coherent thought fizzle. Fine motor control was gone, baby, gone.

The snow had started again, and Jimmy was of course bitching and moaning about being cold, which was almost a boner killer, but not quite. When the key finally slid home, Mike let out a whoop of victory and kicked the door open wide.

The view of the ratty motel room was admittedly a bit of a letdown, but, hey, they were both still pretty drunk.

"Mike?" Melinda said, staring inside.

"Yeah, baby?"

"Is your brother going to his room?"

"This is his room," he said, squeezing her ass for emphasis.

"Then ... where's our room?"

"Right here."

She pushed him away, mid-neck kiss, and stared at him very seriously.

"What's the problem?" He managed, trying to dodge serious and make his way back to Foreplayville.

"Stop it. What I think is happening better fucking not be what is actually happening."

Mike stared at her, feeling incredibly slow. "What?"

"There's only one fucking bed in there, Mike."

Mike grinned. "Shit, how many do you think we need?"

Melinda crossed her arms and backed away from him. "I don't know what kind of person you think I am."

Mike looked from her to Jimmy and it finally dawned on him. "Oh, shit. Him? No! Don't worry about him. He sleeps in the bathtub."

Melinda's face dropped in abject horror.

"No, no, no! Listen to me. I know how that sounds, but it's his choice."

Melinda looked unsure, but Jimmy said, "I like bathtubs."

She looked back to Mike. "His mom dropped him on his head in a bathtub. Ever since, that's the only place he'll sleep. I don't get it, but it's his thing."

Jimmy nodded and shrugged.

Once they were inside, Mike set Melinda up with a drink and walked Jimmy to the bathroom. After insisting the big man brush his teeth, Mike gently helped Jimmy into the tub and then handed him his threadbare Teddy bear.

"You good, buddy?"

"I got it, Mike. Really."

Crouching beside the tub, Mike said, "Then let me hear it back."

Jimmy said, "'Go to sleep.'"

"Right."

"'Stay asleep.'"

"Yep."

"'Don't come out 'til you say.'"

"Because?"

"Cuz some things you can't unsee, Mike."

"That's right, pal. Good night."

Jimmy nodded and Mike pulled the shower curtain closed. He turned out the light. On his way out of the bathroom, Jimmy said, "Mike?"

"Yeah, buddy?"

"You're welcome."

Mike laughed and closed the door.

Melinda had turned the lights off, but she had the TV on. The sound was turned down, but Mike thought he recognized the movie. Some old comedy from the early '60s. Black and white. In the shifting patterns of light and dark, he is very aware of the soft, feminine silhouette in his bed.

He turned away and carefully slid off his jacket and shoulder holster. He folded the cloth over the gun and set it carefully on the rust-colored easy chair in the corner before returning to sit on the edge of the bed. Her arms were around him, then, nimbly working his buttons and slipping the shirt off. Her small, cool hands slid over his back and he was as self-conscious as ever when she felt the thick, raised scars there. Her fingers hesitated for the briefest of seconds, then slowly traced the jagged lines. Then he felt her lips there, soft and hot, and turned to meet them with his own.

18

Jimmy lay curled in the tub, eyes closed tight, the lids fluttering rapidly. Cocking his head, he listened to them through the thin wall, and slowly he smiled.

19

Mike woke with a start, his world transforming in an instant from the warm embrace of darkness to a stark, cold brilliance that was as painful as it was offensive. He shaded his eyes against the day and tried to adjust to the brightness, with very little luck. He did see Jimmy's big feet on the stained carpet, though, and, to them, he said, "What are you doing out here, Jimmy? Where's Melinda? Bathroom?"

"She's gone," Jimmy said.

"What? What time is it?" he asks, but realizes abruptly that Jimmy can't read the analog clock on the wall. He grabs the clock radio on the nightstand. 1:36.

"Did you turn off the heat?"

Jimmy shook his head.

"Fuckin' cold. Is she coming back?"

Jimmy shook his head.

He almost asked for clarification, but realized it didn't matter. He liked her, but since when had that mattered? There wasn't going to be wedding bells, no matter what.

"I guess that's good. Never been much for goodbyes. What else did she say?"

Jimmy shrugged and said, "I didn't talk to her."

"Then how do you know she's not coming back?" There was the tiniest little flutter somewhere inside, and it pissed Mike off. The chance that she might come back shouldn't have made him feel that way. It shouldn't have made him feel anything at all.

"Cuz she took all our money."

"What?" Mike sat bolt upright, ignoring the agonizing headache and lurch of his entire digestive tract.

He spent the next several minutes finding his clothes, climbing into them, and then checking the bathroom anyway in the unlikely event that Jimmy was wrong.

He wasn't.

"That little bitch," Mike said. He turned, grabbed his jacket from the chair and suppressed a sigh of relief at finding his pistol still there beneath it. As he shrugged into the holster, he yelled, "Get some clothes on. C'mon."

"What are we doing?" Jimmy said.

"Getting our money back."

Leaving the room, Mike was nearly to the stairs leading down to the parking lot when he half-turned to tell Jimmy to be sure to put his hat on. In that slight turn, he caught a brief peripheral glimpse of someone peering into their car windows. He reached out to stop Jimmy, but the combination of the kid's forward momentum and Mike's panicked reach resulted in a straight arm blow to Jimmy's solar plexus. Mike heard the whoosh as the breath left Jimmy's lungs and the sharp intake of breath that signaled he was about to cry.

The guy in the parking lot had already abandoned their car and was running, leaping two and three steps at a time, up the stairs toward them, grinning all the while.

Mike knew the grin, and the psychotic fuck to whom it belonged, far too well.

He ran, grabbing Jimmy by the arm and half-dragging him along. They were five feet from the corner of the building when Mike glanced back to see Ash reaching the top of the stairs. He took the corner fast, too fast for Jimmy, who hit the balcony with all his weight, making the metal rail clang. Somehow, somewhere along their brief run, Jimmy's hand had found Mike's. He squeezed now, but in pain or desperation, Mike didn't know. Mike hit the stairs on the other side of the building and rolled his ankle on the second step. He was tumbling, struggling to keep to his feet, and only Jimmy's grasp kept him from diving headfirst to the pavement. At street level, they picked up speed, though Mike's ankle was screaming and starting, already, to swell. They crossed the lot and dove through the rows of decorative bushes demarcating the edge of the property.

There was a street there, little more than an alley, and, on the other side, an abandoned apartment building. Though the walls were crumbling, they would provide at least enough cover to give them a chance to catch their breath, maybe double back for the car.

Mike was dragging Jimmy across the street when he heard something that sounded like a firecracker and a bit of brick exploded from the wall in front of them.

He immediately fell into a defensive semi-crouch and hurried through the abandoned building's open doorway. Glancing back, he saw Ash's arm extended, saw the silenced MK in his hand.

Stairs lead up to the second floor, a death trap, and there's another door, but it leads to the front, the main road. Too open, they'd be fish in a barrel.

Beneath the stairs, though, was a small storage area partitioned off with a thick rusted metal cage. It was dark there, and the detritus of years of neglect provided a decent enough cover. They squeezed in together, and Mike saw Ash enter the room just as he pulled his fingers free of the wire partition. He slowly put his hand over Jimmy's mouth and spared a glance at his friend. The kid was seriously panicking, cheeks flushed, eyes wide and wet. He didn't deserve this shit. Neither of them did. Motioning for Jimmy to stay quiet, Mike slowly took away his hand from Jimmy's mouth and carefully slid his pistol from the shoulder holster.

"Mikey?" Ash said, and Mike felt Jimmy tense violently beside him. He wanted to reassure the kid, but he didn't move. Couldn't move. Kept his eyes on the expensive loafers only a few feet away, his finger trembling on the trigger.

"I sure hope you can hear me, Mikey. All Mr. Bishop wants is for you to return what's rightfully his. That, and a little chat with you, buddy. Hell, he might even be willing to give you a reward. He's a reasonable man, Mike."

Ash bent suddenly, studying the dust patterns in the floor, and Mike nearly put a bullet through his temple. Mike watched him from the darkness, watched the man's eyes trace some perceived tracks to the stairs. He stepped silently to the base of the stairs, head craned back, looking up.

"Don't be stupid, Mikey. I like a good road trip and all, but enough is enough. I want to go home. Only he's not going to let me come home until I bring you two with me. You know how he can be."

Mike and Jimmy looked at each other as they listened as Ash climbed to the second floor. Tiny tendrils of dust whirled down with each creaking step. Above them something fell with a crash, followed almost immediately by the sound of a gunshot. Something fell with a wet splat outside their hiding place, tufts of bloody hair extending from a nearly unrecognizable little body. Mike winced as he realized what it was, what Jimmy was seeing.

"Oh, for fuck's sake," Ash screamed above them. "Now look what you made me do. I shot a cat because of you. Why don't you guys do the right thing and come out? You're making this way harder than it has to be."

Mike chanced a quick glance at Jimmy only to find him squeezing his eyes shut tight. Tears had escaped anyway, and they spilled over his reddened cheeks. Mike held his breath, and the silence there was a tangible, living thing. He could hear his heartbeat, of course. But he could hear Jimmy's, too. And beneath that, an unnatural stillness.

For perhaps the first time, the pistol felt heavy in his hands. Uncomfortable.

Ash had always been a little prick, and Mike would've been lying if he said he hadn't fantasized about shooting him from time to time, but the reality of the situation was something different.

Hurting people? He'd always been good at hurting people. He didn't like it, but it was something he did well. Killing was something different, something he was happy to say he knew nothing about. And if he shot Ash, he would have to shoot to kill.

What if, after all this time, murder was his true calling? What then?

Sweat was dripping into his eyes, burning them, and he wanted to blink it away but he couldn't see Ash, couldn't hear him.

"Have it your way," Ash said, his voice close again. His expensive loafers passed their hiding place on their way back out to the street. Mike watched him go. Ash stopped in the doorway to pop his collar against the cold, and then he was gone.

Mike let out a slow, shuddering breath and put his hand on Jimmy's shoulder. The kid was still crying, silently, God love him. Mike put a finger to his lips as a reminder to be silent, and they waited.

After a time, Jimmy's tears stopped and his eyes drifted closed. Mike recited baseball stats silently to himself to pass the time. Once the sun was down, he slipped out of the storage compartment, favoring an ankle that was still very tender, and did a little reconnaissance. When he was satisfied that Ash was truly gone, he woke Jimmy gently.

"It's all clear. Let's go."

Jimmy climbed out of the cramped storage compartment, but his extremities had fallen asleep and it took several painful minutes to massage the blood back into them. Mike could see that the larger man was tired, hungry, and nearly to his breaking point. They'd been there together more times than anyone should.

"Mike?" Jimmy said as Mike tried to rub the feeling back into his feet.

"Yeah, buddy?"

"Do you think cats go to heaven?"

The question threw him for a second, but he said, "What kind of god wouldn't let cats into heaven, Jimmy?"

"I dunno."

"All right, then."

Once Jimmy could walk, they walked. Mike didn't want to tell him that he had no idea what to do next. No money, no car, no nothing.

"What about our stuff?" Jimmy said, and Mike had to wonder if the kid had been picking up on his doubts.

"We gotta leave it for now. Ash will sit there for a few days waiting for us to come back. We can't afford that."

Jimmy stopped.

Mike said, "It's only stuff, buddy. We'll get more. Down the line. You know we will."

"But my new clothes. My bear."

And here was where he drew the line. The fuckin' Teddy bear?

"I'm telling you, forget it. You wanna get caught? You want things to be like they used to be?"

"No."

"Okay, then. I'm all you got, pal."

Jimmy kicked an empty beer can on the sidewalk and said, "You're not all I got."

"Oh, you think you can make it on your own?"

Jimmy shrugged. "Maybe that's not what I'm talking about."

"No?"

"No."

Mike snorted. "You don't even know what you're talking about."

They walked another quarter-mile before finding a gas station. Inside, the clerk read his newspaper while they pretended to shop long enough to warm up a bit. Then Mike took Jimmy to the counter, to the case where the scratch-off lottery tickets were kept.

Jimmy wasn't on his game, he seemed millions of miles away, but he did his part, concentrating, and pointed at a garish green and silver roll of tickets.

"Seven-Up. But it's the third one in, and it's only for $50." He shuffled his feet a minute, then added, "I gotta go to the bathroom."

Mike turned to the clerk, who was now staring at them instead of his paper. "You got a bathroom?"

The clerk made a vague gesture toward the back of the store. Without a word, Jimmy hurried that way and Mike told the clerk, "Lemme have three of these Seven-Up tickets."

20

Jimmy went down the checklist in his head. He'd done "his business" as Mike liked to say. And he flushed. And he was washing his hands now as he went down the list. He caught his reflection in the mirror and grinned.

He left the bathroom and looked toward the counter where the man with the newspaper was. Then he looked around the store, up and down the aisles, even. He ran to the man with the newspaper and even said excuse me and everything, and when the man asked him what he wanted he asked for his friend. For Mike. Only the man with the newspaper said that he'd bought his ticket and won some money and then left.

LEFT?

Jimmy remembered to say thank you but then he ran out of the store, even though the man with the newspaper was calling after him.

The parking lot was empty, and there was snow everywhere and it was cold. The streets were busy, though, and the cars speeding past were enough to give Jimmy a headache in the place where he often got headaches, this spot at the base of his skull that made his eyes go funny and his neck get stiff. And that was what was happening right then, his eyes were starting to go funny, with weird colors that came out of everything, and his muscles were tightening. And with his muscles he could feel his heart tightening, too, and beating real hard. Hard and fast, making him want to breathe hard and fast to try to keep up, but the cars kept zooming and the snow kept falling and someone was honking and it was all too much.

A car jumped over the curb and screamed into the parking lot, or that's how it seemed to Jimmy. The front of the car, the grill, he remembered, looked like a big, mean smile, like the way kids used to smile at him when he was little. Like Mr. Bishop smiled sometimes, when he thought Jimmy didn't see. And in that car were a bunch of guys. Not men, but not kids. And even through the windshield he could see the stuff. The what-did-Mike-call-it? Oras? The funny lights around things, when his head got bad.

These lights looked red and brown and thick, and he could see things that looked almost like lightning bolts coming out of them, shooting toward him and he was sure scared.

He wanted to run only he didn't know where to run and he wanted to hide only there wasn't no place to hide, only snow and noise and muddy lightning and the pain that was growing. And those boys was laughing and they was pointing. That was at least something he was used to. That was at least something he could tell himself he didn't mind, even though he did. The heat from his neck was spreading, growing up into his head and into his eyes, which were so hot he thought they might explode, only then his cheeks were wet and he had to touch them to make sure it wasn't blood but it wasn't. Just cryin', cuz that's all his crybaby self knew to do. The boys was still laughing and he could hear the laughter of all the others, all of them, over the years, the people who done all the laughins all the time.

Then there was a hand on his arm and he looked and saw it was Mike!

"Aw, his boyfriend's back!" one of the kids in the car yelled, and the others laughed even more.

"Why don't you get the fuck out of here before I make you my girlfriend, eh, you little shit?" Mike said. The kid who was driving got out quick, his face frowny and red, and the waves of stuff in his ora were black and sharp. The other kids started to get out, too, only Mike opened his coat and showed them his gun and Jimmy saw their colors change and even the color of the one kid's pants changed in the front. They sped away even faster than before.

"C'mon, kid, let's get out of here," Mike said. Then he saw something behind Jimmy and moved to grab it. Jimmy had a long tail made out of the toilet paper from the bathroom and Mike fixed it. He felt embarrassed, but more than that, even, he felt happy because Mike was there.

"I'm sorry, Mike. Don't ever do that again. Please never leave again. You're all I got and I'm sorry."

His face, when Jimmy looked at him, was funny. Sad and kinda like he'd done something wrong. He was shooshin' Jimmy the way he always did when Jimmy was crying, but then he said, "C'mon, the cab's gonna be here any minute."

21

The same bartender was polishing glasses behind the bar at the Velvet Kitten, and she appeared to recognize them when they approached.

"Back for more cream sodas?" she said.

"Actually, I'm looking for Melinda." Mike said.

"Ain't here."

"Is she off today?" Mike said.

She shook her head. "Quit this morning."

Mike looked at Jimmy, caught the final flutters of his eyelids as he read her. Jimmy opened his eyes, looked at Mike, and nodded.

"You know where she lives?"

She shook her head.

"Where's your boss?"

She gestured toward the back of the club, near the emergency exit. "He's busy, though."

Mike was already walking back there, with Jimmy a few feet behind him. "You're gonna wanna stay back, pal," he said, then kicked the office door open.

The manager was every strip club manager Mike had ever seen. Fifties, overweight, too much pomade sculpting what remained of his thinning hair into a style that hadn't been fashionable in Mike's lifetime. Yellow eyeglasses that magnified his look of surprise cartoonishly. Cowboy shirt. Jeans down around his ankles so some poor young stripper could service his tiny, semi-functional pecker. He jumped to his feet as the door bounced off the wall loudly, seemingly forgetting where his genitals were. Then he screamed, as surprise and fear caused the woman to clamp down.

"FUCKIN' BIT ME, BITCH!" he screamed.

The dancer gave him a look that seemed to say What the fuck do you expect, dickhead.

Tucking his wounded manhood back into his jeans, the manager said, "Who the fuck are you motherfuckers?"

Mike opened his jacket, exposing the pistol in its holster. "I'm Mister Manners, come to collect for the swear jar."

"What the fuck is this?" the manager said.

"Just need a moment of your time. Preferably alone."

"Did Gattano send you?"

Mike shook his head.

Seeming to relax slightly, the manager turned to the dancer and told her to get out.

"What about my fifty bucks?" she asked.

"You're lucky I don't charge you, you dumb bitch. You almost bit my cock off."

The girl pushed past Mike and Jimmy huffily.

"I'm looking for a waitress who was here last night. Melinda?" Mike said.

The manager looked at him with a vacant stare. "You a cop?"

Mike shook his head.

"Well, sorry to tell you this, but she's gone. Quit."

Mike nodded. "I heard. Where does she live?"

"How the fuck should I know?"

Jimmy stepped forward. "Because you been there before."

The manager started to deny that, but something in Jimmy's stare got to him. Mike didn't even have to pull his gun.

"It's ... fuckin' Island Cove apartments. 6A. Probably not for long. She said she won the lottery and was looking to get out of town for a while."

Mike looked at Jimmy, who only nodded.

Mike leaned over the desk and said, "Say, pal, what kind of car you drive?"

The manager frowned and said, "I got an El Dorado, why?"

"Afraid I'm gonna need those keys. Now."

The manager looked from Mike to Jimmy and back before sighing deeply and slapping his keys on the desktop.

"Thanks. Now close your eyes until I tell you it's okay to open them."

As the manager did so, they backed out of his office without a sound.

22

They were ten minutes down the highway when Jimmy said, "Mike? Could you help me?"

"Helping you is my life, chief."

"I meant with something else."

"Like what? You want pizza? Candy? That shit's gotta wait until we get our money, buddy."

"I thought..." Jimmy said, staring out the window at the passing cars. "I thought maybe you could help me find a girl, too.

Mike took the exit that would get them to Melinda's apartment. At the stop light, he said, "What are you talking about?"

"Like you and Melinda."

Mike laughed. "Me and Melinda? Melinda's a thieving little bitch. You really want that in your life?"

Jimmy stared at him with unreadable eyes. "Mike, I want to find someone, too."

Mike couldn't hold his gaze. He looked back to the road, the traffic, and said, "Man, I don't know."

"I'm old enough to have a girlfriend."

"Yeah, no, it's not that, Jimmy. I guess I don't get why. Girls are a pain in the ass, man. You don't need that shit."

"You did."

"Yeah, well, your old buddy Mike is weak, that's all I can say about that."

The car was quiet for several minutes, then Jimmy said, "I want for once to feel it, too."

"Feel what?"

"Like ... Like what you and Melinda were doing."

Mike turned to look at him again. "Like what we were doing when?"

"Last night."

Mike could feel the heat in his face. "Oho. Oh, you little shit. Don't make me sorry I didn't leave you back at that gas station. Are you fuckin' kidding me?"

Jimmy looked at his feet. "I wanted to know what was so important to you."

"This is fuckin' great."

"It is?" Jimmy said, smiling.

"No, Jimmy, I'm being fucking sarcastic. That's when you say something you don't really mean but you say it like you mean it."

"What?"

"Stay the fuck out of my head, Jimmy. I mean it."

The car was silent except for the sound of the heater, which sputtered and rattled like some dying animal. Jimmy looked out the window. Mike drove. The quiet was a nice change.

The snow-covered sign to the apartment complex read, "Island Cove. Where every day is a tropical paradise!"

Once at Melinda's apartment, Mike peered through the window. He saw stacks of cardboard boxes, newspaper, rolls of shipping tape. There was no movement inside, though. No sound.

He checked the door and, though it was locked, found the knob astoundingly easy to pick. Slipping inside, he gestured for Jimmy to stay put and stay quiet while he searched the place. With luck, he could grab their money and get out without an ugly confrontation.

A quick walkthrough confirmed his suspicions. She was out, but whether she was carrying boxes to her car or out on an errand, he didn't know. He checked under her bed and in the bedroom closet for their bag, but it was nowhere to be found. He was on his way back to what looked like a spare bedroom in the back of the apartment when he heard a door behind him creak. He turned in time to see the baseball bat as it hit him in the forehead.

23

He woke, tied to a chair.

Jimmy was there, free, smiling.

"What the fuck, Jimmy? Why didn't you tell me she was in the closet?" he asked, his head swimming.

"Because we're going to help her."

Mike took a breath to speak, but the movement sent him back into the blackness.

24

Later that night, after a hot shower, a change of clothes (Melinda's ex's, it turned out), a long talk, and a longer drive, the three of them arrived at a shopping mall. The lot was packed, and Melinda and Jimmy followed Mike as he parked the El Dorado in a spot near the road but concealed by a hedge. Mike used a handkerchief to carefully wipe down the steering wheel and door handles.

"Your prints are on file, too, eh?" Melinda said as he got in the back seat of her car. He met her gaze in the rearview mirror. "They got mine, too. What'd they get you for?"

"Something I'd rather forget," Mike said. "You?"

"Same. Maybe I'll tell you sometime." She offered an unexpectedly warm smile. One he wasn't remotely interested in accepting.

"Can't wait," he said.

She turned around in her seat to face him. "Hey, no hard feelings, eh?"

He couldn't help but notice the way the seatbelt slid between her breasts, drawing her shirt tight, emphasizing them. He fucking hated being a man sometimes.

"Easy for you to say. Nobody hit you with a bat."

She shrugged and said, "Sometimes a girl's gotta do what a girl's gotta do."

Mike leaned back and glanced at Jimmy in the passenger seat, in another world, watching the snow fall.

"So let's do this and get it over with."

Melinda drove. She put on a playlist on her phone, a weird mix of music. Madonna, The Stooges, The Smiths, Muddy Waters. Mike found himself wanting to ask her about it, but he didn't. She hit him with a fucking bat. That was the important part of the story, not her eclectic taste.

After an hour or so spent jumping highways and staring with amusement at the truly weird shit playing on the radio, he said, "Where the hell are we going, anyway?"

Jimmy said, "Pittsburgh."

Melinda smiled and said, "That's right! Did you read my mind again?"

Jimmy ignored her and said, "That's where Agnes lives."

Melinda laughed and clapped her hands.

"And who's that?" Mike said.

"My ex's mother. I never would've dreamed of asking her directly, but with Jimmy here, I don't have to."

"Nope," Jimmy said, smiling with satisfaction. The two of them were really enjoying this shit.

Mike, on the other hand, had a headache and his ankle was still throbbing like a bitch.

"Hey, you gonna give us our money back when your little detour is over?"

Jimmy was already nodding. "Yes, Mike. We got it all worked out."

"You do, hunh."

"Yes. Once we're done in Pittsburgh, I'm going to give Melinda some winning lottery numbers. And she'll have a permanent address and nobody will be looking for her and she can be happy."

"Sounds great, if you could do it."

"Of course he can," Melinda said. "He told me how you guys have been managing."

"Sure," Mike said. "But those are scratch-off tickets. Jimmy can't see the future. He can only see what's already there. Sometimes we gotta hit two or three different places to find a winning ticket. Bet he didn't tell you that."

Her enthusiasm took a solid hit. Now she had doubts. That made Mike happy, but he still couldn't stop.

"And another thing: did he tell you about this?" Mike leaned forward and stuck his pinky in Jimmy's ear. The kid protested, but Mike held up his finger to show Melinda. It was covered in bright blood.

"W-What is that?" she said, eyes wide.

"That is what happens when he does it too much. Like now. Jimmy, here, is trying his best to impress a lady, but the fact is that if he does this shit too much, it'll kill him."

Melinda looked at Jimmy. Concerned. Hurt. "Why didn't you tell me, Jimmy?"

Jimmy looked away. Mike could tell that he was on the verge of tears.

He let out a breath and leaned back in his seat again. It seemed to him like he had a real gift, these days, for being the bad guy.

"He didn't tell you because he doesn't understand. His whole life, nobody's cared about him. They care about what he can do. More specifically, what he can do for them. He wants to be liked, to be loved, so he does it. Even if it hurts."

The girl was seemingly stunned to silence. Black Sabbath's 'The Wizard' faded into The Clash's 'Train in Vain' and the windshield wipers swept away the fat flakes that splattered on the windshield.

Mike caught sight of her reflection again in the rear-view mirror and saw that she was silently crying. Bat or no bat, he couldn't handle watching a woman cry.

"You didn't know," he said, to no effect. "Listen, Melinda. I'm sorry. That was harsh, okay?"

By the time 'Me and Bobby McGee' by Jerry Lee Lewis came on, Mike was spilling it all.

"So ... This guy I used to work for, back in West Virginia. Maybe you've seen him on TV, if you're awake at three in the morning, flipping channels. Pastor Art Bishop, Abundant Life Ministries?"

He looked to her, expecting recognition, receiving none.

"No? It's one of those 'megachurches'. Bishop's written a ton of books, got the TV thing goin' on. Fucker owns two private planes."

Melinda wiped her eyes.

"Anyway. Jimmy's mom was a parishioner. A true believer, you might say. Bishop was known for faith healing, speaking in tongues, you name it. Most of it was carnie tricks, not that she knew that. She'd accidentally dropped her baby in the bath, y'see, and she believed that Pastor Bishop could make him right again. But once he figured out Jimmy's gift? Shit, he didn't want him back to normal. Jimmy was proof, as far as he was concerned, that there really was something more to the world, y'know? So he put Jimmy to work. Behind the scenes. He didn't wanna share the spotlight, y'know. Plus, well, Jimmy's not exactly the face you put on God."

Jimmy turned and smiled warmly at Mike. It nearly broke his heart.

"I had a past, y'know, but I tried to put that behind me, get back on my feet. Bishop used Jimmy to find people like me. We were good security and we worked cheap ... once we knew that Bishop had info nobody could possibly have on the shit we'd done. Shit that could put people like me away for a real long time.

"I started out as one of Bishop's personal security team, but I hit it off so well with Jimmy that he 'promoted' me. It was me and a guy named Ash. Little prissy fucker, but mean. See, when Bishop needed a bit of Jimmy's 'holy spirit' to wow the sheep, he didn't give a shit what the effect was on Jimmy. He started getting sick. Lots of headaches, stopped eating. Ash's job was to push Jimmy when Jimmy didn't want to continue. He was killin' the kid, and he didn't care. So a couple months ago, I took him. Bishop's been looking for us ever since. If he finds us, I'm pretty sure he'll kill me and put Jimmy back to work until he can't work him anymore."

Melinda was crying again, and when she faced Jimmy, he said, "Can we get pizza now?"

25

"That was good," Melinda said, looking at the demolished pizza on the table.

"Try eating this crap every day for months."

"Seriously?"

"It's all he'll eat."

Melinda looked over her shoulder at Jimmy, who had begged them for quarters to play the old pinball machine in the back of the restaurant. He played the game with his entire body, jumping and leaning as the ball careened through its courses, shouting as it fell into the gutter.

"I guess you love him like a brother, don't you?"

Mike looked away. "I don't have any brothers. I'm not always the best guy in the world with him. But I love him, yeah. Why else would anyone eat this crap every day?"

Melinda laughed, and the sound of it made him smile.

"He's lucky to have you," she said.

"Me? No. Half the time I want to cave his skull in. Half the time I'm wondering what the hell I thought I was doing when I took him out of that church. I didn't have a plan, didn't know what it would be like, y'know? Then I think that he could be listening in, and I think about how that would kill him."

Melinda stared at him for a long moment, her eyes lingering on his. "I've been thinking. Maybe I should drop you guys off somewhere and head back home."

"Why? Jimmy likes you. He wants to help you. You should let him."

"I don't want to hurt him anymore."

"I'll be there. I'll keep an eye on him. You ready to get back on the road?"

She nodded. When they got up to retrieve Jimmy, they saw that his eccentric style of play--and his high score--had attracted other customers who had gathered around the machine to cheer him on. They groaned in disappointment as Jimmy told them that he had to get going.

26

The game was easy, easier by far than some of the convoluted shit Bishop had Jimmy do. They go to the nursing home a little after two in the afternoon, unfortunately just in time for Agnes's nap. The orderlies brought the clearly perturbed old woman into the common room, where Mike and Jimmy waited on a couch covered with ancient crocheted afghans. They smiled and waved at her as she entered the room.

"Hi, Agnes," Mike said. "It's Mike and Jimmy, your cousins from California. Do you remember us from Bruce's wedding?"

"No, I do not," Agnes said. Puzzled, she looked for her escorts, but they were already gone.

Mike's smile broadened. "Well, that's too bad. We sure remember you, don't we Jimmy? How's Bruce doing? Still living in Buffalo?"

"No. He got divorced from that woman. Moved back here, about a year ago. What did you say your names were?"

Without missing a beat, Mike said, "So sorry to hear that. How's little Chelsea holding up?"

"Fine," the old woman said. "Better, if you want to know the truth. Getting away from that horrible mother of hers was a blessing. Terrible business, that."

Mike glanced at Jimmy, whose face was slack, blank.

"Are you in town long?" Agnes asked.

"No, I'm afraid not. Just stopped in long enough to see you."

Agnes raised her thin eyebrows. "Really?"

"Yep. Whattaya think, Jimmy, have we seen her long enough?"

He nudged the kid, who jumped as if startled. "Hunh? Oh. Yeah. It's 3212 Eastman Avenue. Monroeville."

The old woman stared at them, sputtering, "Why, that's Bruce's address! You said you thought he was in Buffalo! Who are you? What is all this?"

Mike got up and leaned over to hug the old woman. "It was so nice to see you, Agnes. You take care now."

Mike guided Jimmy toward the door as the old woman was struggling to her feet. "Come back here," she called. "I'm calling the orderly. These men are not my cousins!"

27

From inside Melinda's car across the street, the three of them watched her ex-husband, Bruce Matthews, emerge from his house and head up the block. He was a decent enough looking guy, Mike thought. A far cry from the sort of guys Melinda had surrounded herself with at the Velvet Kitten. At least this guy owned a suit.

"So that's him, eh?"

She nodded. Her eyes were shining, wet.

Bruce stopped at the corner and chatted with the few other people gathered there. A middle-aged woman in yoga gear had brought her dog. The paunchy, balding guy had a stroller. The three of them seemed happy to see each other.

"Can you tell what they're saying?" Melinda asked.

Jimmy nodded and closed his eyes. "Talking about their kids. The lady with the dog is bragging about her son getting a big role in the school play."

"What about Bruce?"

Jimmy's eyes fluttered. "Chelsea is taking ballet. She has a recital next week."

Melinda wiped at her eyes. "What else?"

Sweat had begun to form on Jimmy's forehead, but he laughed.

"What's funny?"

"He's proud of her because she made the honor roll, but he's also proud of himself for not saying that in front of the guy with the stroller because he knows that guy's daughter gets bad grades and is always in trouble."

Melinda laughed, and Mike even joined in. The situation wasn't funny, really, but the tangible relief he felt from Melinda was almost his relief, too. The tears rolling down her cheeks were happy tears, at least. He took his handkerchief and offered it to her.

A yellow school bus arrived. As the doors opened and kids started spilling out, Melinda leaned forward anxiously.

Chelsea was the last kid to get off the bus, and Melinda became very still.

"Want me to tell you what he's thinking now?" Jimmy asked, breaking the silence.

"I want to know what she's thinking."

Mike touched Jimmy's shoulder. "You okay?"

Jimmy nodded, but he winced a little as his eyes began to flutter again.

Bruce knelt to scoop up his daughter in a hug. After putting her back down, he took her hand and they started to walk back to their house.

"She's ... happy.

Melinda faced him. "She is?"

"Yes. She has ballet practice today, and she loves ballet. She's a little scared about her recital, but excited, too. She had a pretty good day at school, but lunch was yucky. And there's a boy in her class named Derrick. He's mean to her and she doesn't know what to do about it."

The man and his daughter reached the house and went inside.

Jimmy gasped as he opened his eyes. "That's all I can get. I'm sorry."

A trickle of blood leaked from his ear.

Melinda touched the side of his face gently. "That was enough. Are you okay?"

Melinda wiped her eyes again and took a deep breath. Mike watched her, and he watched the way Jimmy watched her. The kid was looking at her with a kind of longing Mike had never seen from him. Then his features clouded, he frowned, and cried out, "NO. You can't do that!"

Melinda jumped back as if shocked, remembering too late that he could read her mind as well.

Mike leaned forward again and said, "What, buddy? She can't do what?"

Jimmy was rocking a little in his seat, and a thicker stream of blood leaked from his ear.

"She wants to leave! Leave, without even talking to Chelsea. Without even trying. She thinks she can't make her any happier than she already is."

Mike looked at Melinda and saw it was true. It would've been easy to get pissed off, thinking that they'd spent hours packed in the car for nothing. Mike wasn't pissed, though. He got it. Sometimes being the good guy meant eating a shit sandwich, taking a hit, however much it sucked, however much it hurt. Sometimes being the good guy meant doing all of that with a smile, even when you felt like you were dying inside.

"She could be happy with you, Melinda," Jimmy was saying. "She's your daughter. She loves you. And it's your dream. You've been thinking about this day for a whole year, and I made it happen for you. I made your dream come true. And now we're going to get Chelsea and ... and the three of us can all go away together. And then Mike can go away like he wants to."

Mike felt a twinge in his stomach. A sick twist.

"Jimmy. C'mon, man. I don't want to go away," he said, and it didn't even sound convincing to his own ears.

"Yes, you do."

"No, I don't." A little better, but still piss poor.

"YES YOU DO, LIAR. I BREAK RULE NUMBER ONE ALL THE TIME."

The sheer violence of Jimmy's yell startled him. Mike couldn't think of anything to say, could barely even take a breath. He stared at Jimmy's face, at the deep hurt and betrayal he saw there.

When Jimmy spoke, he carefully enunciated his words. The sharp staccato rhythm of them was designed to hurt. Sounds as little bullets. "I hear what you think. I know the truth. The only thing you want, the thing you think about more than anything is how to get rid of me. 'Jimmy the Freak.' That's what they called me in school, but it's what you call me in your head. I was trying to help you. To make it easy for you."

It was then that the big man broke into great, gasping sobs. Mike took his handkerchief back from Melinda and used it to wipe Jimmy's eyes, though he protested. Outside the car, a speed walker broke stride to stare at them through the window.

"Drive," Mike said.

Melinda looked back at him. "What?"

"Drive before somebody here calls the cops."

The speed walker was approaching fast, bending down to look closer at them.

Melinda threw the car into gear and sped out of the neighborhood, barely sparing a glance for the house where her daughter lived.

"Where am I going?" she asked.

"Anywhere. Just out of here. Fast."

"Then where?"

"I don't know. Drop us off at the first crappy motel you see. Oh, for fuck's sake, Jimmy."

He was balled up now in the front seat, pulling as far away from both of them as he could. The tears, the sobs, wouldn't stop.

"Leave him alone," Melinda said. Something was there in her voice that Mike didn't much care for. Judgement. As if she was any better. The last thing he needed was any shit from her.

The car grew silent, except for the sounds of Jimmy crying.

28

Mike stared at the sign lighting up the night. Lighthouse Motel. Which was weird because they weren't anywhere near the ocean.

The kid was doing his best to ignore Mike. Instead he was watching the snow fall. He'd watch it all day if nobody told him to do anything else. More fuckin' snow. Mike hated the snow. Sure it looked pretty the way Jimmy was watching it, but by morning it would be shitty gray slush fuckin' up the roads.

He saw Melinda come out of the office, and he watched her walk over. He got out to meet her.

"What are you gonna do about him?" she asked.

Mike looked back to see that Jimmy had fallen asleep with his cheek pressed against the window. "Guess I'll get the tub ready and come back down to wake him up."

She smiled, which struck him as odd, but she held out the key on its neon pink fob, and he took it.

After getting the bathroom ready he returned to the car and gently opened Jimmy's door. Slowly, catching the kid as his body started to spill out. "C'mon, bud. It's bedtime."

He helped Jimmy to his feet. Jimmy yawned and mumbled, "Whattaboutthesnowman?"

"Tomorrow, maybe."

"But you always say tomorrow."

Once Jimmy was settled in the tub, fussing momentarily as he remembered that he didn't have his Teddy bear, Mike pulled the shower curtain closed and turned off the light. Melinda was standing near the door, awkward. Expectant.

He approached her and said, "So I guess this is goodbye. I don't know if I'm supposed to give you a hug or shake your hand or what, but if you start, I'll follow your cues."

It was meant to be a joke, but Melinda's smile faded.

"What?"

"What what? You gotta get back home, right? And we gotta keep moving on. Tomorrow I gotta figure out some new transportation, but we don't have long before he finds us again, and I don't want you here when that happens."

Her eyes narrowed. "I never took you for a coward."

"I'm not a fuckin' coward."

"Really? You're running, aren't you? Aren't you dragging a mentally handicapped man all over the country, using his gifts to steal so you can keep running? Sounds like a coward to me. Didn't you say this guy will never quit chasing Jimmy?"

Mike didn't say anything, but he looked away. He wanted a drink.

"So that's your great plan? To keep running? How is being on the run with you better for Jimmy than the life he left? Why don't you make a stand?"

"There is no stand, Melinda. Bishop is really good at what he does. He's got shit on everybody. And it's not like he's overtly blackmailing them. He expects people to tithe, and they do. Half the fucking police department makes monthly donations. If there was something to be done, don't you think somebody would've done it? The only thing that would stop him is--" He met her gaze, saw the hope in it, then looked away again. "--is something that I'm not willing to do.

Not that I could even get close enough, if I was. A month or so before Jimmy and I took off, Bishop lost his mind. He became certain someone was going to kill him, so he upped security. Started wearing a bullet proof vest. Had fuckin' metal detectors installed around his compound and the church. He'd put Jimmy on overtime, had the kid scanning the entire congregation, looking for his would-be assassin. I'm amazed nobody's taken a potshot at the old prick, frankly. I keep checking the news, hoping, but nothing. Trust me, I want nothing more than to stop running."

"Then we'll think of something else," she said.

"There's no we here. It's tough enough keeping Jimmy safe. I can't watch both of you."

"I didn't ask you to." She took a step closer to him. Mike never thought he was the smartest guy in the world, but he wasn't a dumbass, either. He knew what she was trying, and he wasn't going to fall for it.

He was, however, only a man.

She leaned in close, her lips brushing his. He could smell her perfume faintly and feel the heat radiating from her.

"We're the same, you and me," she was saying. Her hands were on his chest, and, somehow, his hands were on the small of her back.

"A couple of fuck-ups trying to make amends. And we keep on fucking up."

"That's bullshit," he managed with difficulty, as her body pressed against his.

"That's not what Jimmy says."

"I never told him that."

"You didn't have to."

Mike pulled away from her, a sudden surge of anger taking over from other, baser instincts. Melinda laughed.

Grinning Mike said, "You think that's funny? Did I mention that he was reading you and me the other night?"

"You mean when we were...?"

He nodded.

She blushed.

"Not so funny anymore, hunh?"

She glanced at the bathroom. "But he's sleeping now, right?"

"Like a baby."

She stepped closer and leaned in for a kiss, but Mike stepped back and shook his head.

"Listen, Melinda ... I don't know if you know how hard it is for me say, but you gotta go. Go home."

Her expression was unreadable as she backed away, toward the door. As she retrieved her purse, she opened it, removed a thick envelope, and tossed it to Mike. He looked at it briefly "Your money," she said.

Mike tossed it back, then said, "Keep it. Don't go back to that job. Or that apartment."

With a half-smile she said, "How will you find me?"

Mike smiled back and said, "I got Jimmy, don't I?"

"Tell him thank you for me. Please. It's like a weight's been lifted from my soul. That might sound corny, but it's true. And I ... I hope you can feel that way, too, someday." Mike held out his hand for her to shake, but she hugged him fiercely instead.

As she left, he said, "I'll see you around, maybe."

She nodded, then turned away to disappear in the night and snow.

29

He woke sometime in the middle of the night from an unremembered but pleasant dream to the feel of cold steel pressed against his temple.

"Hiya, Mikey."

Mike could not turn to see the speaker, but he knew exactly who it was.

The only person it could've been.

"Ash," he said.

"Where's the girl?"

"Gone."

"Hope you had fun, Mikey, because it's her credit card that lead me right to you. First the pizza, then the room. Dumb, dumb, dumb. It's not like you to make dumb mistakes like that, is it?"

Mike shook his head as much as he could, thought the barrel of the silencer was giving him a headache.

"Jimmy in the tub?" Ash asked.

Mike nodded.

"Get him up. We have a long drive and I'm in no mood for any more bullshit from either of you."

He eased the gun away from Mike's head and let him sit up.

Mike went to the bathroom. He knew something was wrong before he turned on the lights because it was cold in there. Freezing.

The bathroom window was open. The tub was empty.

Then Ash was behind him and Mike felt a pistol pressed into his kidney.

"Think the girl took him?"

"No."

"Why not?"

"Because she disappointed him the way we all have."

"Awww. Is that supposed to make me feel bad? You better get dressed, Mikey. If you don't find him, I don't have any reason to keep you around."

While Mike was getting dressed, Ash picked up the phone and pressed the redial button.

30

"It's okay if you wanna answer that," Jimmy said.

The phone that lay on the front seat beside the cab driver was not one of the fancy ones that Jimmy sometimes saw on commercials. This was one of the old ones, the kind that you had to flip open like on Star Trek or something.

The driver grinned in the rear-view mirror and said, "No, sir. Good customer like you gets my undivided attention."

Jimmy didn't even have to try to know what the guy was thinking. It was obvious from the way he kept glancing at the meter as it ticked higher. So far, the trip was up to $132, and it kept going up all the time.

"You sure your friend can afford this fare?" the driver asked. He asked every ten miles or so.

"I promise," Jimmy said. "Big tip, too."

"Yeah? How big are we talkin'?"

"How big do you want?"

"I dunno ... a hundred?"

"Sure. He's gonna be real happy to see me."

"No shit? Happy enough to pay two hundred?"

"Sure."

The driver smiled again, to himself, and Jimmy was glad to have a few minutes of silence.

The driver's phone rang again.

31

Ash slammed down the phone.

Mike tried to keep a poker face, but there was something awfully satisfying in watching the little shit throw a tantrum.

Turning abruptly, as if sensing Mike's thoughts, Ash punched him in the stomach. Mike tried to take a breath, to keep his feet under him, but then he saw Ash's arm cock back, followed by a flash of brilliant pain as the butt of the gun met his temple.

32

"And what did you say your name was, sir?"

The secretary was new. Used to be, the front desk was run by ladies in the congregation. That was back before Abundant Life church had grown, though. Jimmy didn't think she looked like the kind of lady that ought to be the secretary for a church. She was too young, too pretty. Her dress showed too much of her boobies, not that Jimmy minded too much himself.

"Pete," the cab driver said.

"I'm sorry, I was speaking to your ... friend."

Jimmy stopped looking where he'd been looking and said, "Just tell Pastor Bishop that Jimmy is here."

"Jimmy who, sir? What's your last name?"

"I ... forgot," Jimmy said. "But Jimmy is enough. You tell him Jimmy's back and I promise he'll know."

The secretary picked up a phone and said something into it quietly. After she hung up, she said, "Someone will be right with you."

"Someone better be," Pete said. "I got an unpaid $500 fare, and that's not including the tip he promised."

"I assure you, sir, that no good shall be withheld from those to whom it is due."

Jimmy saw Pete jump, startled, but Jimmy was used to the way Mr. Long did that. He was a big man. Not as big as Jimmy, but what Mike called "solid." Big as he was, Mr. Long was sneaky. It was like he was always behind you.

"What do we owe you?" Mr. Long was saying. He was smiling, but Jimmy knew that there wasn't anything happy behind the smile. In the times he'd tried reading Mr. Long, Jimmy wasn't sure there was anything there at all. Only cold.

"Fare is five-forty, but he promised me an extra two."

"Will $1000 cover it?" Mr. Long asked, offering a stack of money.

Jimmy watched his stunned driver take it.

"Welcome home, Jimmy. Please come with me, and we'll get you settled in."

Mr. Long smiled again. Jimmy followed the man, hoping that, wherever they put him, they'd give him a blanket.

33

Mike woke to the sound of Ash laughing as he drove. It was the sound high school jocks made when they pantsed some poor nerd in the middle of a crowded hall. With the throbbing roar that currently occupied Mike's skull, the laugh was ample enough justification for him to pound Ash's face into the dashboard until all sound ceased.

Unfortunately, he found himself handcuffed. And in the back seat. And unable to move without wanting to projectile vomit.

"Oh, that's incredible. Yes. We're still about an hour away. Yes. See you then."

Ash hung up the phone and met Mike's gaze in the rear-view mirror.

"Well, you're awake. That's good. Guess what?"

Mike swallowed. His mouth tasted like an old sock. "Jimmy went home."

"Sure did. Must've been some argument you two had." Ash chuckled to himself.

Mike looked out the window, thinking about life and wondering when it had all gone to shit.

34

The room that Bishop had provided for Jimmy was more than generous. He'd paid to have a 50-inch television mounted on the east wall. Several of the newest video game consoles were connected to it, as well as most of the major streaming sites. Toys from years past stood on shelves or spilled from toy boxes. He'd never denied Jimmy anything. It was the least he could do for his little miracle.

And though he'd spent thousands on a hand-crafted race car bed, Jimmy was still insisting on sleeping, as he did now, in the bathtub.

Bishop heard a low beep as the keycard lock on the room disengaged. Mr. Long entered the room and said, "Reverend Bishop, Michael is ready." Nodding, Bishop followed Long out of Jimmy's room and ensured that it was locked.

As they took the elevator down to the basement, Bishop said, "I'd like you to have Nurse Randolph look in on Jimmy. Get him up, fed, and checked out. Then you might send her around to check on our Michael."

Mr. Long nodded silently and took his phone from his pocket, ready to obey. The elevator doors opened on a dimly lit hall. Behind a locked door at the far end, in a room that was little more than a glorified janitorial closet, they found Mike. He was bound to a chair with duct tape, his face swollen and bloody. Ash stood beside him, using a handkerchief to wipe blood from his leather driving gloves.

"Are you ready to repent yet, Michael?" Bishop wondered.

Mike lifted his head and stared at the charlatan, his gaze unflinching despite his injuries. Ash cocked back a fist, but Bishop stepped forward, raising a hand, and said, "Why don't we rest for a few minutes."

Bishop made a slight gesture, and Mr. Long scrambled to retrieve a folding metal chair from the corner. He unfolded it, brushed it off, and set it down before Bishop, who sat and considered Mike for a moment before saying, "I'm thinking, perhaps, that you don't understand how sorry you should be. So let me spell it out for you. Since you took Jimmy, our attendance is down 30 percent. Donations are down 50 percent. I've been forced to cut a third of the staff. I've had to use stooges in order to maintain the illusion that I can do what I can do when Jimmy is with me. Now some of them are blackmailing me. Threatening to reveal my secret. And I'm afraid if we can't get back on track soon, everything will be undone." He smiled a kindly smile, one taken straight from his pastor's toolbox. "Now are you ready to tell me you're sorry?"

Mike only stared at him in disgust.

"You know what your problem is, Mike? I told you back when you first came to see me. Do you remember? Everybody's got what Shakespeare called a 'fatal flaw.' The secret to happiness is to find yours and fix it. And see, this is yours. It's why you are where you are. You don't understand repentance. You don't understand what it means to take responsibility and say you're sorry. And until you say you're sorry, I can't move on to forgiving you. And you can't move on to being happy. And that means we're going to be stuck right here. And I don't think either of us wants that."

Bishop made another almost imperceptible gesture, and Ash's fist slammed into Mike's cheek hard enough to rock his chair, nearly toppling him. The pain and simultaneous sense of falling was nauseating, but his reaction was something he could never understand, something that would bother him later, long after the pain had faded.

In that moment he was sure that he wouldn't leave this room alive. He was certain that they would continue to torture him until he finally gave Bishop his bullshit apology, and then Long, or someone like him, would put a bullet in his head. And if his body was ever found, the world would shrug and continue on without a care.

Except Jimmy.

If he died, what would happen to Jimmy? Bishop would use him until he used him up, and how long would that take? Not long, no.

And in this split-second realization that happened in the time it took for his brain to reboot and check for damage after a particularly good right jab, Mike felt a kind of despair that welled up from deep in his gut, spiraling up his spine and exploding in his fevered brain, a lifetime of regret expressed in a single name, cried wordlessly.

"You can save us all a lot of trouble, Michael," Bishop said, leaning in to pat his knee. "You can end this any time you want, in fact."

Mike had a mouthful of blood that he was tempted to spit right in the bastard's eyes, but he didn't want to get hit again. He'd seen so many movies that seemed to teach the way to act tough, but he knew now that those movies were lies. He didn't have that iron will, and there wouldn't be some last moment rescue anyway. There was only him and them and pain, and he didn't want to hurt anymore. His lips twisted, trying to form the words that tasted like bile in his throat.

"Pastor Bishop," Mr. Long said, his voice urgent. Mike turned to look at the man, though the movement sent the room spinning again. Long was on his cell phone, and the expression on his face was one of panic. "It's Jimmy ... Something's wrong with Jimmy."

Bishop stood. Looking at Ash, he said, "Keep an eye on him, but keep your hands to yourself."

35

It was easy to underestimate him, to forget his size. It was easy to see him as a child and not a fully-grown man. Until he went berserk, that is.

By the time Bishop and Long took the elevator back to the third floor and made it to Jimmy's room, the shattered television had been torn from the wall and thrown into the hallway, barely missing the nurse. Jimmy had apparently torn down his curtains and, seeing the cinderblock wall where a window should have been, impaled a bean bag with the curtain rod, sending a blizzard of polystyrene pellets swirling through the room. Every shelf had been torn down, the bureau dismantled, and the expensive game systems smashed.

And the screams. Incoherent, inconsolable.

"Jimmy, what in God's name are you doing?"

Whirling on the pastor, Jimmy screamed, "HE'S NOT SUPPOSED TO BE HERE!"

Bishop swallowed hard. "Who, Jimmy?"

"YOU HURT HIM. STOP HURTING HIM."

Bishop could see in Jimmy's eyes that he knew, but, even having seen the boy's powers, he could hardly believe it. Lying would be pointless.

"Calm down, Jimmy. We can figure this out."

"You stop hurting Mike or I'll never do anything for you ever again." Jimmy said quietly, his voice quavering with rage.

"Jimmy, I--"

"I know what you're thinking. I know what you planned to do, but you better not do it. You better let him go right now."

Bishop raised his hands in a slow, placating gesture. "Jimmy, you know I can't do that. What if I brought him to you instead? Would that be okay?"

"Don't HURT him anymore."

"Nobody is hurting him, Jimmy." He nodded to Mr. Long, who left to retrieve Mike. "And now that I've done something for you, I need you to do something for me."

From the hall, the nurse approached with a small syringe in hand.

"NO MEDICINE!" Jimmy bellowed.

"Jimmy, please. You're upsetting yourself," Bishop said.

"No."

Bishop sighed softly. "If you insist. But we have a busy day tomorrow. Lots of catching up to do."

Surveying the damage, Bishop clucked his tongue in disapproval as Ash and Mr. Long arrived, dragging Mike between them.

They put him in the unused bed, shoving aside pieces of broken shelving to make room. After Mike was situated, Bishop joined Ash and Long to guide them out.

Jimmy heard the lock beep as it engaged. He rushed to his friend."

"Mike, are you okay?"

Mike groaned. "Am now, pal. Thanks."

"You're not supposed to be here."

"Couldn't leave you with that asshole, could I?"

"You'll ruin everything."

"What are you talking about?"

Jimmy frowned, stooped to pick up a stuffed bear from the floor, and said, "Nothing. Let me think."

With that, he went into the bathroom and slammed the door.

36

Jimmy got used to his new schedule very quickly. After breakfast, they'd come for him. Mr. Long would escort him down to a small anteroom next to Pastor Bishop's prayer room. Inside, Jimmy saw the decorative mirror in the prayer room was a mirror only in there. In this little room it was a window, and he could see everything that went on in there. Jimmy thought that trick was both pretty mean but also kind of cool.

On this particular day, an old lady walked in to meet with Bishop. Jimmy didn't like her. She looked like a nice old lady at first, but there was something mean and ... not right in her eyes.

They were talking about stuff, but Jimmy wasn't sure what it was because he was fixed on her and concentrating. It felt almost like popping a bubble, and once he was through the bubble he would hear her. Getting through was getting harder, though. He didn't tell anybody that part, not even Mike, but it was. He could feel himself sweating, shaking, as he pushed and at first, he thought that maybe he wouldn't be able to do it this time. But then with a whoosh he made it through and felt the old lady's thoughts swarm around him.

"No fancy talk, Pastor. I told you what I want, and I expect to get it." The old lady, Jimmy saw now that her name was Eunice Elkind, said.

"My dear, I thought we had a deal."

"Deals change," she said.

Jimmy wasn't sure what they were talking about, but then he saw them meeting one morning before a service. He saw Mr. Long pay her. Then he saw her pretending to get healed during a service at Abundant Life.

Then he saw something else, something she kept in the back part of her memories, the place where people kept things they didn't want anybody to know.

Jimmy said, "Her first husband. Name was Earl. She poisoned him. 30 years ago. When the poison only made him sick but didn't kill him, she fed him soup to make him feel better only when he was eating it she hit him in the head with a skillet."

Mr. Long listened, smiling. He spoke into a small microphone, one that Jimmy knew went to a small, flesh-colored earpiece in Pastor Bishop's ear, and said, "She murdered her husband, Earl, 30 years ago."

Jimmy wiped the blood from his ear.

Inside the room, Mrs. Elkind said, "You think the police wouldn't want to know what kind of church you're running?"

Bishop smiled and said, "Oh, I think they'd be much more concerned about what happened to your faithful husband Earl, one fateful morning 30 years ago, don't you?"

She paled visibly, almost the way characters did in the old cartoons Jimmy liked. "But ... h-how do you...?"

"That doesn't really matter now, does it Mrs. Elkind?" Bishop asked. "Am I correct in assuming that this ends our ... what did you call it? Renegotiation?"

Mrs. Elkind's hand was at her throat, trembling. "O-of course."

"And may I suggest that you pass along a word to all your friends who are considering a similar course of action. Don't."

The lady left on shaky legs, and Jimmy watched Bishop stand, happy with himself, and run his hand through his hair.

To Mr. Long, Jimmy said, "I need to talk to Pastor Bishop."

"Not right now, Jimmy. He's very busy."

"Now. I need to see him now."

Long put a hand on Jimmy's shoulder and squeezed just a bit too hard to be friendly. He said, "Very soon. He doesn't need you for a little while. Why don't we go back to your room, and I'll order you a pizza?"

Jimmy knew it wasn't really a question, so he let Long take him back to his room.

Things were mostly back to normal there. Bishop had people come in to fix or replace the broken things, but this time the TV he gave Jimmy was small. He wouldn't get a big one until he knew he could trust Jimmy again, Pastor Bishop said.

As they came in the room, Mike stood to meet them. The swelling was gone, but his face was all bruised, and Jimmy thought it had to hurt way more than Mike said it did.

"How much longer are you going to keep us here?" Mike asked.

Mr. Long didn't say anything, but Ash came in from the hall. He was wearing his leather gloves again, and that was enough to make Mike back away and not ask any more questions.

They left and the lock beeped.

Jimmy sat down at the small table and opened his pizza box. "Want some?" he said to Mike. Mike just shook his head.

37

The following week, in the church office, Mr. Long said, "It seems that your meeting with Mrs. Elkind worked. The others have withdrawn their requests."

"Things are looking up," Bishop said.

Mr. Long handed Bishop a piece of paper and said, "I took the liberty of putting together this e-mail we'd like to send out detailing what we're calling 'your incredible recovery.'"

Bishop scanned the text and chuckled. "'After 40 days in the wilderness.' I like that."

"As you can see in the second paragraph, we're letting parishioners know that a special blessing is in store for those who bring a friend with them to church this Sunday to hear the whole story."

"This looks fine. Go ahead and get it out. And let's put the phone banks on extra shifts for the rest of the week. Use this as the basis for the script."

Mr. Long nodded. Then, taking a stack of note cards from his pocket, said, "And this is a preliminary draft of your sermon based on your notes."

"I'll take a look at that as soon as I can. Anything else?"

"Jimmy keeps saying that he needs to talk to you."

Bishop frowned. "What does he want?"

Mr. Long shrugged. "Says he'll only talk to you."

"Christ. All right. I've got a meeting in an hour. That shouldn't last long. Then lunch." Bishop stopped to think. "What time does Jimmy eat?"

"12:30."

"I'll take it to him. I haven't had pizza in a while, and it'll be a nice surprise, don't you think?"

38

Jimmy was sitting on the floor, watching cartoons, when the lock beeped. He got up, surprised to see Bishop in the hall behind Mr. Long and Ash. Ash entered the room and set Jimmy's usual pizza on the table. Jimmy glanced at Mike, who watched Bishop's men the way a whipped dog regards its abusive owner.

Bishop walked in, followed by Long and said, "Hello, Jimmy. Bob tells me you want to talk to me. I thought we could do it over lunch."

"Not here. Not like this."

"Oh, Come on, Jimmy. I brought your favorite." Bishop leaned over to open the pizza box. Jimmy picked up the box and threw the pizza at Ash, who dodged most of it and stared at Jimmy with such unveiled hate that for a moment the boy was afraid.

"Not here," Jimmy yelled. "It's private, and when somebody has to talk to their pastor, they don't do it over pizza."

Ash sneered and tried to brush the pizza remnants off his shirt.

Bishop watched Ash before pointing to the mess on the floor and saying, "Clean that up."

Ash crouched and shoved the ruined pizza back into the box. As he did, Bishop said, "Jimmy, whatever you have to say to me can be said in front of everyone here."

Jimmy's face crumpled. "No it can't. And besides, how many things I done for you? How many? I can't even count anymore. And then I came back here all on my own. And then I helped you with that old lady. And now I want this one thing and you won't do it. Well if you won't do it then ... then I'll read all of you until my ears bleed and I die. Is that what you want?"

Bishop calmly said, "Don't talk such nonsense."

"Not nonsense. Take me out of here right now."

Bishop took a deep breath, let it out slowly and nodded to Mr. Long, who used his card key to open the door. Ash kept cleaning the pizza. As they left, Jimmy looked back at Mike. He wanted to smile for his old friend, but the door closed before he was able to.

39

Bishop, Mr. Long, and Jimmy went down to the church office. Once there, Long said, "Do you want me to stay?"

Bishop shook his head. "No, that's all right. Tell Lisa you need to use her office. You can wait in there."

Long nodded and gave Jimmy an unreadable glance before leaving the office. Bishop closed the door and turned to see Jimmy at the window, looking out at the fresh gusts of the snow storm that had plagued them all week.

"It's pretty," Jimmy said.

"Yes," Bishop said. "I suppose it is. Now we're alone. As you asked. What's on your mind?"

Jimmy turned away from snowy view, toward Bishop. "Let Mike go."

Bishop's face was a mask of sadness. "I can't do that."

"He knows what you know about him," Jimmy said. "He's not going to tell. He won't do anything to stop you. He was only worried about me. And I'm here. To stay."

"Do you really mean that?"

"Let him go and I'll do whatever you want for as long as you want. Okay?"

Bishop gave the appearance of considering it. Finally, he said, "Okay."

"But I know what you're thinking. You can't tell me you let him go and then have Mr. Ash take him to the canal."

The color drained from Bishop's face. In a world full of carnival tricks and cheap sleight of hand, it was occasionally easy to forget that Jimmy was the real deal. "Of course not," he said.

"Do we have a deal?"

Bishop said, "Is that all you want?"

"No. Mr. Long has to give Mike some money. And I want to see you let him go. I want to wave to him. Goodbye."

Bishop crossed to his desk, and pushed the buzzer on the intercom.

Jimmy faced the window again, watching wispy snakes of snow slither across the street.

Mr. Long entered. Bishop hurried to him and spoke low enough that Jimmy couldn't hear.

Jimmy's brow furrowed, and he wiped at his ear vacantly.

"Are you serious?" Mr. Long asked.

Bishop nodded and returned to whispering.

"No," Jimmy said loudly. "Make it $3000."

Bishop straightened. He exchanged glances with Long, then looked to Jimmy with a forced smile. "Well now, Jimmy, I don't know if we have that kind of cash on hand."

Jimmy tried not to smile as he said, "You do. In your safe. The one behind that picture over there."

Bishop swallowed hard. He whispered something else to Mr. Long, who glanced again at Jimmy before leaving.

Bishop turned and smiled again. "There, see? All done."

"Not yet. I told you I want to wave goodbye."

Bishop crossed the room to stand beside Jimmy. Even patted him amicably. "We can do that from right here."

Jimmy nodded.

Bishop checked his watch. "Can we talk about what else is on your mind while we're waiting?"

Jimmy shook his head, eyes on the street below.

The sun peeked out from behind the clouds. It almost hurt Jimmy's eyes to look down there, the brilliant light reflecting off the snow. But then there was Mike. He stepped off the sidewalk, into the street, and crossed to the other side before turning to face the windows. Mike looked at the church and hesitantly waved, but Jimmy wasn't sure if Mike could see him or not. Jimmy waved anyway, his eyes burning.

"Satisfied?" Bishop asked.

Jimmy nodded as the first tears fell from his eyes. Then the grief welled up in him, escaping in a sob. Arms extended, massive hands opening and closing like a toddler's, he said, "Hug me, please."

Bishop stared at him in disgust. The ruddy face streaming tears and snot. The open, shameless display of raw emotion. It embarrassed the pastor, but this was hardly the first time he'd feigned sympathy.

"For heaven's sake, Jimmy," Bishop said, stepping into the embrace. Jimmy hugged him tight.

Too tight.

"Jimmyy," Bishop managed before realizing that he couldn't draw in another breath. His chest was completely compressed, ribs screaming in protest, lungs burning. He tried again to speak, assuming that the poor, stupid hulk simply didn't know his own strength, but all he could say was, "J-CH-CH-CH-CH."

And then, as the first of his ribs snapped, he knew.

Eyes bulging, lips tingling, he knew.

Flapping like a flounder, feet kicking at Jimmy's shins, head thrashing, the primitive part of his brain seeking any way to make.

This.

Stop.

He knew.

He could hear the photos and mementos on his desk, useless things, shattering, but all of that was nothing. The most important thing in the universe, more important even than breathing, was the slow surge of pain that flared from between his shoulder blades, sharp and bright and so very hot. As a boy, as a man, he had often wondered what the final moments of life would be like, whether one's life flashed before their eyes or not, and what lay on the other side of a person's last breath.

With a loud pop, Bishop knew.

40

Bob Long took a few deep breaths to collect himself after letting Turner go. The little shit should've been in a shallow grave now, not walking the streets with last week's collection take in his pocket.

And yet, these were strange times.

He'd long ago given up any delusions about an invisible man in the sky who grants wishes sometimes, but he couldn't for the life of him explain Bishop's little pet. And if Jimmy the Freak was real, well, maybe he needed to take the rest of the bullshit seriously, too.

He rounded the corner to Pastor Bishop's office and heard glass break.

Moving quickly, Long threw open the door.

Jimmy sat on the edge of the mahogany desk, crying as he looked down at the limp, broken body he cradled on his lap, the body of Pastor Bishop.

"Now it's over," Jimmy said, looking at him with red-rimmed eyes.

Long took an involuntary step back, swallowing hard, and fumbled for his phone.

41

Mike was skeptical of his freedom. He half-expected to see Ash waiting for him, around the corner from the church. But he wasn't. So far, so good.

Still, he had the sense that the other shoe hadn't dropped quite yet.

And then came the sirens.

As an ambulance raced by, followed by several police cars, Mike said, "Oh, fuck. Jimmy, what did you do?"

He turned and ran back toward the church.

By the time he got there, out of breath and ready to puke, they were loading a covered gurney into the back of the ambulance. No lights, no sirens. Not anymore.

Still out of breath, Mike tried to ask the attendants what had happened, but nobody would answer.

Then a couple cops came out of the church. They were escorting Jimmy. He was in cuffs.

Mike's heart sank.

But then Jimmy looked at him, right at him. And he smiled.

Like an angel, he smiled.

42

"**M**r. and Mrs. Turner, thank you so much for coming," The doctor said. Colby, the name tag on the white coat said. "I'm sorry that it's taken us so long to reach this point. The state doesn't exactly make it easy for visitors, even when the visitors are family. In your case, well..."

And that could have meant any number of things, Mike supposed. That they weren't family. That they'd looked into his criminal record. That they'd looked into Melinda's.

It was a gray day. November, and the first snow of the year. A sky the color of dryer lint. Snow falling, fat flakes dusting the coils of razor-wire atop all the fences.

He took Melinda's hand, squeezed it. She squeezed back.

That they'd found each other again was amazing. That things had turned out how they had? The whole thing reminded him of Jimmy's lottery trick. This time, though, he'd picked the jackpot winner.

Colby led them inside, past the nurse's station.

"Now," the doctor continued, "before I take you to the visitation area, I'd like to make one small request."

"What's that?" Mike said, stepping aside for a nurse with a cart.

They moved on, walking through a sunny common room filled with patients in clean, white gowns. Several watched Sesame Street on an old console set, staring slack-jawed at Muppets on the screen. Some did crafts. Some stared out the windows.

"When Jimmy first arrived with us, he was convinced he was special. That he had the power to read minds."

"You ever tell him to prove it?" Melinda asked.

One of the patients smiled at them and pointed toward something in the courtyard.

"Of course. It was important for him to confront reality. And of course he couldn't do it, so he tried to rationalize it. He said he'd been able to do it before. In particular, he said that he used to read your mind all the time. And that you knew about it."

Mike looked out the window to where the patient had been pointing. He saw a few guards first. Then, two perfectly rolled balls of snow. One on top of the other. A headless snowman.

Then, there was Jimmy, dressed in white like the other patients, rolling a head-sized ball of snow between his reddened palms. He carefully stacked it on top of the others, patting it until it was just right.

The doctor said, "It's taken six months of intense therapy and psychotropic medications to move him past this delusion. And I have to ask that you not mention it during your visit today. I'm afraid if you do, the setback might be cataclysmic. Can I count on your help?"

The patients at the window cheered at the completed snowman. Jimmy looked at them with his goofy crooked grin and waved. They waved back.

"Of course," Mike said, a lump in his throat.

"Thank you. Now if you'll follow me please. Let's go say hello, shall we?"

Jimmy closed his eyes, tilted his head back and opened his mouth.

There's something almost magical about it, Mike thinks, watching the fat flakes of snow appear from the lint gray sky. The snow was really starting to come down, swirling in thick spirals around the snowman. And then there was Jimmy. Way too old to be catching snowflakes. But that's what he's doing.

And he's grinning.

THE END

ABOUT THE AUTHORS

CHARLES COLYOTT lives on a farm in the middle of nowhere (Illinois) with his wife, 2 daughters, cats, and a herd of llamas and alpacas. He is surrounded by so much cuteness it's very difficult for him to develop any street cred as a dark and gritty writer. Nevertheless, he has appeared in *Read by Dawn II*, *Dark Recesses Press*, *Withersin* magazine, *Horror Library Volumes III & IV*, *Terrible Beauty*, *Fearful Symmetry*, and *Zippered Flesh*, among other places. He also teaches a beginner level Tai Chi Ch'uan class in which no one has died (yet) of the death touch. You can get in touch with him on Facebook, or email him at charlescolyott@gmail.com. Unlike his llamas, he does not spit.

MARK STEENSLAND self-published his first book while in fourth grade and has been telling stories ever since—some of them true. He became a professional journalist at the age of 18, writing about movies for such magazines as *Prevue* and *American Cinematographer*. His award-winning films have played in festivals around the world. His novel for young readers, *Behind the Bookcase*, was published in 2012. He currently lives in California with his wife and their three children.

There's a monster coming to the small town of Pikeburn. In half an hour, it will begin feeding on the citizens, but no one will call the authorities for help. They are the ones who sent it to Pikeburn. They are the ones who are broadcasting the massacre live to the world. Every year, Red Diamond unleashes a new creation in a different town as a display of savage terror that is part warning and part celebration. Only no one is celebrating in Pikeburn now. No one feels honored or patriotic. They feel like prey.

Local Sheriff Yan Corban refuses to succumb to the fear, paranoia, and violence that suddenly grips his town. Stepping forward to battle this year's lab-grown monster, Sheriff Corban must organize a defense against the impossible. His allies include an old art teacher, a shell-shocked mechanic, a hateful millionaire, a fearless sharpshooter, a local meth kingpin, and a monster groupie. Old grudges, distrust, and terror will be the monster's allies in a game of wits and savagery, ambushes and treachery. As the conflict escalates and the bodies pile up, it becomes clear this creature is unlike anything Red Diamond has unleashed before.

No mercy will be asked for or given in this battle of man vs monster. It's time to run, hide, or fight. It's time for Red Diamond.

Available in paperback or Kindle on Amazon.com

http://bit.ly/DiamondUS

THE SPECIMEN (THE RIDERS SAGA #1)

From a crater lake on an island off the coast of Bronze Age Estonia...

To a crippled Viking warrior's conquest of England ...

To the bloody temple of an Aztec god of death and resurrection...

Their presence has shaped our world. They are the Riders.

One month ago, an urban explorer was drawn to an abandoned asylum in the mountains of northern Massachusetts. There he discovered a large specimen jar, containing something organic, unnatural and possibly alive.

Now, he and a group of unsuspecting individuals have discovered one of history's most horrific secrets. Whether they want to or not, they are caught in the middle of a millennia-old war and the latest battle is about to begin.

Available in paperback or Kindle on Amazon.com

http://amzn.to/1peMAjz

WELCOME TO THE BLACK
MOUNTAIN CAMP FOR BOYS!

Summer,1989. It is a time for splashing in the lake and exploring the wilderness, for nine teenagers to bond together and create friendships that could last the rest of their lives.

But among this group there is a young man with a secret-a secret that, in this time and place, is unthinkable to his peers.

When the others discover the truth, it will change each of them forever. They will all have blood on their hands.

ODD MAN OUT is a heart-wrenching tale of bullies and bigotry, a story that explores what happens when good people don't stand up for what's right. It is a tale of how far we have come . . . and how far we still have left to go.

Available in paperback or Kindle on Amazon.com

http://bit.ly/OddManKindle

ON THE HORIZON FROM
BLOODSHOT BOOKS
2019-20*

The October Boys – Adam Millard

Dead Sea Chronicles – Tim Curran

The Hag Witch of Tripp Creek – Somer Canon

Behemoth – H.P. Newquist

Dead in the U.S.A. – David Price

Blood Mother: A Novel of Terror – Pete Kahle

Not Your Average Monster – World Tour

The Abomination (The Riders Saga # 2) – Pete Kahle

The Horsemen (The Riders Saga # 3) – Pete Kahle

* other titles to be added when confirmed

BLOODSHOT BOOKS

READ UNTIL YOU BLEED

Made in the USA
Lexington, KY
15 November 2019